The Phantom Killer

The rediscovered cases of Sherlock Holmes Book 4

Arthur Hall

Paperback ISBN 978-1-78705-233-8
ePub ISBN 978-1-78705-234-5
PDF ISBN 978-1-78705-235-2

Published in the UK by MX Publishing
335 Princess Park Manor, Royal Drive,
London, N11 3GX
www.mxpublishing.co.uk

Cover design by Brian Belanger
www.belangerbooks.com and www.redbubble.com/people/zhahadun

Arthur Hall was born in Aston, Birmingham, UK, in 1944. He discovered his interest in writing during his schooldays, along with a love of fictional adventure and suspense.

His first novel "Sole Contact" was an espionage story about an ultra-secret government department known as "Sector Three" and was followed, to date, by three sequels.

Other works include four "rediscovered" cases from the files of Sherlock Holmes, two collections of bizarre short stories and two modern adventure novels, as well as several contributions to the continuing anthology, "The MX Book of New Sherlock Holmes Stories".

His only ambition, apart from being published more widely, is to attend the premier of a film based on one of his novels, possibly at The Odeon, Leicester Square.

He lives in the West Midlands, United Kingdom, where he often walks other people's dogs as he attempts to create new plots.

The author welcomes comments and observations about his work, at arthurhall77777@aol.co.uk

By the same author:

Sole Contact

A Faint and Distant Threat

The Sagittarius Ring

Controlled Descent

The Final Strategy

Facets of Fantasy

Curious Tales

The Plain Face of Truth

The Demon of the Dusk – A first rediscovered case from the files of Sherlock Holmes.

The One Hundred per Cent Society - A second rediscovered case from the files of Sherlock Holmes.

The Secret Assassin – A third rediscovered case from the files of Sherlock Holmes.

CONTENTS

1 A Tale of Deception

2 The Second Victim

3 Great Trees Manor

4 A Visit to Pentonville

5 A Warning

6 A Respectable Citizen

7 The Sirius Club

8 Sea Hill Cemetery

9 Miss Elizabeth Jervis

10 Danger in Transit

11 An Uncertain Death

12 A Nervous Client

13 A Last Revenge

Chapter One - A Tale of Deception

In my accounts of my long association with my friend and colleague, Mr. Sherlock Holmes, I have often commented on his apparent indifference, except when they presented him with an intriguing problem, to the fair sex. Indeed, he displayed little interest when I announced my own impending marriage, other than to express a measure of disappointment. The sole exception, of course, was the adventuress Irene Adler, whom Holmes invariably referred to as *The* Woman.

Naturally, in the course of our adventures, other women appeared and as quickly were gone. These rarely evoked emotion of any kind in my friend, save one who, until now, I have not mentioned in my writings.

It was, I recall, a bright early summer morning when our landlady, Mrs. Hudson, showed a rather downcast but extremely attractive young lady into our sitting room.

"My dear Holmes," I said before she advanced, "I did not know that you were expecting a lady."

"I was expecting no one." he said with a casual air.

"Yet your expression suggested no surprise."

He sighed as he rose from his armchair. "Come, Watson, you know my methods well enough by now. It was simply a case of listening, since the sound of a man's footsteps on the stairs would have been very different."

I had no time to consider my embarrassment at failing to recognise this most obvious indication, because my friend had already crossed the room and was guiding our guest towards the vacant chair. After introductions, we sat in front of the empty fireplace. Her name, she told us, was Miss Juliette Villiers, and she lived with her widowed father in Mayfair.

"I cannot help but observe that you are suffering some distress," my friend said to her at once. "Perhaps you will allow me to order some tea or coffee, while you compose yourself. We can then examine your difficulty at our leisure."

She lowered her head, staring at the floor. "No, no thank you, sir. I fear you will not look upon me so kindly when you have heard me out. It is shame that has brought me to you."

Holmes frowned, and regarded out visitor critically. "Very well, Miss Villiers, pray tell us what has led up to your coming to us. I should add that, if it is comfort that you need, a priest or relative could well be a more appropriate choice."

She looked directly at us for the first time. "You do not recognise my name from the newspapers?"

"The pages which usually concern me have made no mention of it. All I know of you at this moment is that you are of French extraction and have recently been engaged to be married. That the arrangement was cancelled, and that you are the daughter of a doctor."

Her mouth opened slightly as she sat astounded at Holmes' deductions. I reflected that I had seen such an expression on many faces, over the years.

"I can see how my name suggested my ancestry, Mr. Holmes, but your further reasoning is quite beyond me."

"I seem to recollect your name in a *Standard* article," I interjected. "It did indeed describe the end of a betrothal, to a Mr. Morton Janner, I believe."

Her face coloured slightly, as she replied. "Our separation was the result of my foolishness, and when my indiscretion was brought to light."

"Miss Villiers, so far you have spoken in riddles," Holmes said with a trace of impatience. "Please take a moment to collect your thoughts, and then relate to us what has occurred in the correct order. Pray be precise as to details. Leave out not the smallest feature."

"I did indeed leave my fiancé," she began, avoiding our eyes. "Less than a week before the wedding I ran away to Scotland with a man who had bewitched me. He said that he wanted us to marry, but one night he returned in a rage from a gambling house and from his actions then I knew that our union could never be."

Holmes' expression made his disapproval evident. "Did this man mistreat you?" he asked.

At this, Miss Villiers drew back her sleeve, to reveal dark bruises along much of her arm. "He beat me, because he lost a large sum at the tables. I am covered in bruises. I could not contemplate living a life where my safety and happiness were dependent on his whims."

"He has used you most cruelly," I commented, while Holmes was silent on this aspect. I sensed that, to some extent, he felt that she deserved her punishment.

"What then, do you wish us to do?" he enquired.

"That will become apparent, sir, when you have heard the remainder of my tale."

Holmes fixed her with an icy glare, and I expected at any moment that he would declare that she was wasting his time. In the small silence that followed, I heard a hansom or cart rattle along Baker Street as the morning sunshine made patterns on the carpet before me. I looked at my friend expectantly.

"Pray proceed," he said at last.

"The next time Mr. Stephen Golding, for that is his name, left me in our room alone, I fled. I caught the first train back to London and was reunited with my father. He was unhappy but he did not judge me, for I am his only daughter and only living relative since the death of my mother. The scandal, he said, would subside in time."

"Was it at that point that Mr. Janner ended his engagement to you?"

"He did, as soon as he discovered the reason for my sudden disappearance. I suppose I cannot blame him."

Holmes did not disagree and regarded her, I thought, with some distaste. "Presumably, there is more to this revelation?"

"I am grateful for your patience, Mr. Holmes," Miss Villiers murmured. "I think you will now see why I have chosen to consult you, for that was not the end of the matter regarding Mr. Golding. He followed me to London and became a consistent nuisance until three days ago, when he was found murdered."

My friend returned her glance indifferently. "A man of that sort invariably has disreputable associates. Any of them could have been responsible. His death need not be connected with you."

"That is also the conclusion of Scotland Yard, and so after a single interview, I have been left alone. However, my former fiancé has been less fortunate."

Holmes was becoming restless. He got to his feet and wandered over to the window. After a short appraisal of the scene below, he turned back to Miss Villiers.

"Are you saying that Mr. Janner has been arrested?"

"That is so. It happened shortly after Mr. Golding's body was discovered."

"So you would have me prove his innocence, if indeed this is possible? Have you considered that he may actually have committed this crime? Jealousy is a compelling force."

"I knew my husband-to-be well. He would never have done this. Murder is not in him."

"He did not, as things turned out, know *you* as well," Holmes reminded her, "but I will make my own decision as to his guilt."

4

I saw her relax slightly, because he had indicated that he would at least make enquiries.

"I would have expected nothing else. Thank you, Mr. Holmes."

"In the absence of results, that may be premature. Do you know the name of the inspector who conducted the interview with you?"

"I do. It was Inspector Hopkins."

Holmes nodded. "Hopkins is one of the Yard's best. He would not have made the arrest without good cause."

Miss Villiers shook her head. "I do not know what evidence he had, other than circumstance."

"Thank you, Miss Villiers," said Holmes after a moment's thought. "I do not think we need detain you longer."

Her face brightened. "You will pursue this?"

"I have said as much."

"Then I have done all that I can for him."

With that she rose abruptly, and left the room without another word.

"I think you were a little harsh, Holmes," I remarked at the window after we had seen her board a hansom.

"Knowing you as I do, Watson, that does not surprise me. But I will have none of your sentimentality, where women are concerned."

"You have made your feelings clear on that score, before now."

He nodded. "You saw Miss Villiers as a woman deserving of sympathy, worthy of forgiveness perhaps for a single mistake. I

5

saw her as a cold machine, intent only on marrying whoever offered the best for her future prospects."

"Are you forgetting that she came here for the sake of her former fiancé?"

"You believe so? I tell you that she seeks only to rid herself of the guilt she feels, somewhat surprisingly, since her deplorable and deliberate actions indirectly caused Mr. Janner's imprisonment. Did you hear her utter a single word of regret at the heartbreak she undoubtedly inflicted on him by eloping with another, despite the wedding being only days away?"

"I confess that I did not."

"I should have been surprised if you had replied otherwise, since she evidently *does not* regret it. As she saw it, her lover would furnish her with a more comfortable life than that she anticipated with the man she had agreed to marry. This Golding appears to have represented himself as possessing considerable means, whereas in truth he was an opportunist and a gambler. By contrast, I should not be surprised to find that Mr. Janner is an ordinary, hardworking sort -- honest, but somewhat lacking in resources. Miss Villiers spoke of 'a man who bewitched me.' Pah! She saw the opportunity to do better for herself."

He had referred to Miss Villiers as "a cold machine", and it occurred to me then, not for the first time, that the description was not altogether inappropriate for Holmes himself.

"I can follow your reasoning there, Holmes," I volunteered with some pride, "and it is apparent that Miss Villiers is of a quite wealthy family, since her clothes are of expensive quality. I can see how she would wish to maintain her accustomed standard of life. You did not explain, however, your other deductions, such as her being the daughter of a doctor and that she was recently engaged to be married."

He gave me one of his quick, almost sympathetic smiles. "As it often proves to be, Watson, it is simplicity itself. Mingled with the fragrance of what is, I am sure, a most expensive perfume, I detected a faint trace of ether, chloroform or similar anaesthetic. Thus I knew at once that she was connected to the medical profession. Since she is a woman, it is most likely that her position is that of a nurse, yet her unsympathetic and superior attitude precludes it. I cannot see her attending the poor in an ordinary hospital, nor as the assistant of a country physician. Who then would she be more likely to work for but her father, whose practice must be lucrative enough to enable him and his daughter to live in Mayfair?"

As always, I felt ashamed that I had neglected to share his observations.

"But the engagement, and the ending of it?"

"Surely, Watson, you noticed the impression of a ring that remains on the third finger of her left hand. She is not married, therefore the ring signified an engagement. This must be no more, because the ring is now absent."

I said no more on the subject, for it was apparent that his thoughts were already elsewhere. He resumed his place in the armchair and filled his old briar. After he had thickened the air in our rooms with several clouds of smoke, he took his watch from his waistcoat pocket and glanced at it.

I needed no confirmation of the approach of the time for luncheon, as the first pangs of hunger were already making themselves felt.

"I see that we are of one mind," Holmes said as if he had read my thoughts. "We will postpone our visit to Hopkins at the Yard until we have fortified ourselves with Mrs. Hudson's curried lamb. That appetising aroma grows stronger with every passing moment."

Chapter Two - The Second Victim

Hopkins led us along corridors that were dim and cheerless.

"You are quite positive then, of Janner's guilt?" Holmes asked him.

The inspector's serious expression deepened. "It seemed obvious, Mr. Holmes. When I interviewed him I could not help but notice his relief and delight at Mr. Golding's death. Also, I found one of Janner's cuff links at the murder scene. That was my main reason for making the arrest."

"Where was Mr. Golding killed?" I enquired.

"At the Gryphon Hotel, doctor, in Hammersmith. He had taken a room for a few days. I can find no permanent address for him in London, for he seems to have led a nomadic existence. He earned his living, if you can call it that, by gambling. Judging by his hands, he was a stranger to hard work."

"An excellent observation, Hopkins," Holmes remarked. "How did Janner explain his presence in the room?"

Hopkins shrugged. "It surprised me that he did not deny it. He swears that he went to see Mr. Golding to have it out with him about Miss Villiers. The two men fought, and Janner has bruises to prove it. His story is that he gave Mr. Golding a good hiding for ruining his happiness and left him suffering, on the floor but alive."

"And you have no evidence that might confirm that?"

"None. Mr. Golding's body was found in the narrow passage between the hotel and the next building. He had been tortured before he was strangled and thrown from a window."

"Tortured?" Holmes repeated. "How?"

"His face was burned, by vitriol."

"Was any of that chemical found on Janner, or any sign that he previously had any in his possession?"

For the first time, Inspector Hopkins certainty wavered. "I can recall none."

"It is really very good of you, Hopkins, to allow us to see Janner in his cell."

"You have pointed me in the right direction before now, Mr. Holmes, and the Yard has always done well out of your involvement. However, I must accompany you."

"That is understood."

We reached a dim passage with a line of barred doors. Hopkins gestured to an officer who awaited us, and keys were produced. Holmes and I followed the inspector into the narrow stone cell, lit only by a shaft of light from a tiny window high above.

"On your feet, Janner," Hopkins ordered.

The young man who stood up to face us was unshaven and showing signs of great strain. His face was of a sickly pallor and his fear evident.

"Whoever you are, gentlemen, I swear to you that I am an innocent man," he protested in an unsteady voice. "I have killed no one, only beaten the man who took away the woman I loved."

"I am Sherlock Holmes," said my friend. "My associate, Doctor Watson, and I are far from convinced of your guilt. As a consulting detective, do you wish me to conduct an investigation into the circumstances that have brought you to this sorry state?"

I saw hope flare in Janner's eyes, but it faded immediately.

"My thanks to you sir, for your concern, but I am a working man, of little means."

I remembered that Holmes had mentioned that he expected as much, during his observations about Miss Villiers' conduct.

"What, pray, is your occupation?"

"I am a clerk, in the shipping office of Keen Brothers. They are exporters of dry goods."

Holmes nodded, and I saw a flash of satisfaction in his glance. "I do not think you need concern yourself about my fees. It would, however, be of much help to me if you would stretch out your arms to allow me to examine your hands."

Janner looked at each of us in quick succession, with a bewildered expression. Though it was obvious that he did not comprehend the reason for Holmes' request, he held up both his arms for inspection."

"Thank you. Please turn your hands over."

He did so with as little understanding, until my friend gestured that the examination was over.

"I see that Mr. Golding did not fail to defend himself, although you prevailed in the end."

Janner touched his bruised face. "I formed the impression that he had some experience as a pugilist, though not recently."

"That would doubtlessly have proven useful, given the sort of existence he apparently led."

"I cannot understand how Juliette -- Miss Villiers - could have taken up with such a dishonourable man."

"Women do not often think, or reason, as we do," I said from experience.

The prisoner nodded. "As I have discovered."

Inspector Hopkins, who had been silent during the interview, asked. "Is there anything more, Mr. Holmes?"

Holmes had been giving Janner a long appraising look. "I think not, Inspector. For now, I have learned enough." As we turned to leave, he added. "You may take hope, Mr. Janner, from the fact that I believe that there is more to this affair than is evident. I will look into your case, and you will know the results shortly."

I think Janner called his thanks, but his voice was cut off as the guard slammed the cell door behind us. We retraced our steps along the corridor.

"Will you tell me, Mr. Holmes, what I have missed?" Hopkins enquired.

"I will relate to you my observations, for your consideration."

I recalled that Holmes had always considered Hopkins to have some admirable qualities. Far from sneering at my friend's methods, as Lestrade had done at first, he had shown himself eager to learn and to employ imagination as well as logic.

"To begin with," Holmes said, "we have the curious method of dispatch. Does it not strike you as strange, that vitriol was used, then strangulation, before finally throwing the body from the window?"

"This was because of a woman. When a man's anger has its roots in passion, who knows to what lengths he may resort?"

I nodded my agreement, but Holmes, I could see, was not convinced. "I can accept that the motive is a powerful one, but I cannot imagine Janner acting in that manner. After subduing his opponent in a fight, he would surely have simply killed him, if he had a mind to, by either strangulation or hurling him into the alley, not taken the trouble to use vitriol which he happened to have upon his person."

"It is difficult," said Hopkins, "to say what men will do, when the moment arrives for them to decide whether or not to kill. We are arguing in circles."

11

"But then, there is the clear indication of Janner's hands, which make it unlikely that he used the chemical."

"Because they were unmarked?"

"Precisely, Inspector. He would have had to have carried some sort of container which he was obliged to uncork or unfasten, then splash the liquid into Mr. Golding's face. Ask yourself, is it likely that, during or immediately after a violent altercation, that his hand would have been as steady as to avoid marking himself or his clothing altogether?"

We came to a halt, Hopkins with his head on his chest.

"Very well, Mr. Holmes," he said after a moment of consideration, "it can be supposed that there is room for some doubt. Can you offer another explanation for Mr. Golding's death?"

"Certainly," my friend responded. "I believe that he was killed by some other person, an assassin, for reasons we have yet to discover."

"But how have you reached such a conclusion?"

"By searching my memory. I recall that someone of the same name was killed recently in mysterious circumstances. The newspapers had it that an accident had occurred, and I remember pasting the clipping into my index because I found the account unconvincing. My action in preserving it for future reference has now been vindicated, I think."

"If there had been evidence of foul play, we would have pursued the matter."

"I do not doubt it. Tell me, Hopkins, would you have any objection to Watson and myself visiting the Gryphon Hotel, so that I may see the room where Mr. Golding apparently met his end?"

"None at all. Our investigation there has been completed."

"Thank you. It may be that I shall see you soon, probably in the morning."

It was late afternoon by the time the hansom left us outside the Gryphon Hotel in Hammersmith.

I looked up at an unimposing façade, mortar was missing from the brickwork and paint peeled from the entrance door. I reflected that Golding's gambling must have brought him little success of late, despite his representations to Miss Villiers, and I read from Holmes' expression of distaste that his thoughts were similar.

Behind an ancient desk in the lobby a man in a threadbare coat sat reading a newspaper. At our approach he looked up, but said nothing.

"We would like to see the room formerly occupied by Mr. Stephen Golding," Holmes announced.

"Police again?" The man responded. "I thought we had seen the last of you."

"We have come directly from Scotland Yard."

"I see. Very well, then."

I had wondered if, without official standing, we might encounter some difficulty in gaining entry, but the man's assumption settled the matter immediately. He half-rose and stretched out his arm to take down a key from a rack on the wall, pushing it across the desk towards us with indifference.

With Holmes leading, we trudged up the dusty staircase until we reached the fourth floor. The key opened the door easily, and we entered a chamber dimmed by lowered blinds.

He was still for a moment, peering into the gloom before striding over to the window and lifting the blinds. As light flooded in he looked through the smeared glass, down to the floor of the alley.

"A fall from here would be sufficient to break a man's neck," he observed, "without other assaults upon his person. But let us see what this room can tell us, we may be able to reconstruct Mr. Golding's last moments."

With that he whipped out his lens, and began to examine the frayed carpet. "Here," he said from the middle of the room, "is where the vitriol was introduced. There are various spots and splashes across a small area, in a pattern which suggests that the victim was lying down."

"Already unconscious?" I ventured.

"Most probably, or dead. That would have been better for him."

"A horrible fate."

"Yes, indeed." He moved around the furniture, his eyes everywhere. "Halloa, what have we here?"

I watched as my friend picked up several bundles of clothes, apparently screwed into a ball and hidden beneath the bed.

He held them up before him, slowly shaking his head. I could see that some of the garments had been recently pressed. Certainly, they were not meant to be thrown out for street beggars to fight over.

"I marvel that our friends at Scotland Yard have made nothing of this!" Holmes exclaimed.

"It seems that Mr. Golding sought to conceal his morning suit," I observed. "Could it be that he expected these things to be stolen?"

"Perhaps." Holmes approached the large double wardrobe and flung open the doors. Several more coats hung there, including evening wear, which I imagined Mr. Golding would have worn while gambling.

"Whatever he intended to do with his clothes, it looks as if he was disturbed before he completed his task," said I.

Holmes knelt to examine the floor of the wardrobe. I saw that it was covered with fragments of dried mud.

"So," he cried triumphantly, "we now know not only the reason for the displaced clothing, but also that the killer entered the hotel by the side entrance."

"How can you be certain?"

"Simply because the alley running along the side of the building has several patches of thick mud. The killer must have passed through it to leave such a trail. I noticed traces on the stairs and just inside this room, also. There are more here because he waited in concealment for his victim, long enough for some of the mud to dry sufficiently to fall off his boots."

"Do you mean that the killer threw out the clothes in order to make room for himself in the wardrobe?"

"Precisely. He must be a fairly broad individual to have needed to create so much space. He remained hidden while Janner and Mr. Golding fought, awaiting his opportunity to strike."

"We must tell Hopkins at once, and secure Janner's release."

Holmes laughed shortly. "I think the good inspector will require a little more proof than this, Watson. But, let us see if this room can tell us more."

With that he began a lengthy inspection of the bed, the remainder of the floor and the bundles of clothing. When that was done he examined the walls, noting several bloodstains that were doubtless indications of what had occurred during the fight. Finally he returned to the wardrobe, where he plunged his hands into every pocket of the jackets and trousers hanging there.

"Aha!" he cried suddenly, withdrawing a crumpled ball of paper from the tiny ticket-pocket of a tweed coat. "Once more our friends at the Yard fall short."

He spread the paper out, and together we read what was written upon it:

She is gone. I have struck her down. I will come for you soon.

"What can this mean, Holmes?" I enquired.

"It is exactly as I suspected. Mr. Golding was murdered by someone we do not know. Janner is indeed innocent. I mentioned before that the name 'Golding' was familiar to me, and now I am certain that the woman referred to here is the same as in the newspaper article that I remembered. There is nothing more to be learned here, but tomorrow I will seek Hopkins' assistance in gaining access to the Records Room at the Yard."

#

We arrived early. Once more we trod the dull, echoing corridors. Inspector Hopkins was interested in Holmes' discoveries, and eagerly accompanied us to the Records Office. He had the grace to look embarrassed at the Yard's failure to make the same observations, but my friend made no reference to their shortcomings.

"Here we are, gentlemen," the inspector announced as he unlocked a heavy door. "Every case that the Yard has dealt with is represented here."

"Thank you, Hopkins," Holmes said as we entered a long room filled with shelves and cabinets. "Kindly direct me to the files under 'Golding'."

Hopkins took us along a row of cabinets marked with letters of the alphabet. At length he stopped, withdrawing a thick ledger and turning its pages.

"I have it," he said triumphantly. "Three women of that name have come to the notice of the Yard recently. One is dead, the victim in a poison case, while another is behind bars awaiting trial for shoplifting." He closed the ledger after memorising a number and found a folder in a corresponding drawer. "The third will be the one we are concerned with."

He placed the folder on a nearby table and opened it. Holmes and I peered at its contents with him.

"So," my friend said after a moment, "we see that the deceased Mr. Golding had an unmarried sister, Martha. She fell onto the tracks at Paddington Station in front of an oncoming express, no more than two weeks ago."

"It was reported to us by a family friend," Hopkins read. "Inspector Gregson went to investigate on the man's insistence, but concluded that the woman took her own life. A tragic affair."

Sherlock Holmes nodded. "Where was she living?"

Hopkins ran his finger down the page. "Not far away, in a rented room in Fulham. I see your thoughts, Mr. Holmes -- you intend to examine Miss Golding's home. I cannot see that you would learn anything by that, for the room was quickly re-let to a family. Her few possessions were of no value, and were burned."

Holmes considered briefly. "Who was the friend who reported the incident?"

"Mr. Anthony Bersworth, of Great Trees Manor, Camberwell. I take it that you are going to pursue this, Mr. Holmes?"

My friend turned and faced us both, wearing a determined expression. "You may take it that way, Hopkins, for your assumption is correct. It would be easy to dismiss the letter that I found in Mr. Golding's clothes as a prank, but I am quite convinced that he was not the first victim in this affair."

We engaged a four-wheeler immediately on leaving the Yard. For much of the way Holmes was silent. He sat with his chin upon his chest as we journeyed towards the southeast of the city.

"I wonder," he said at last, "whether Martha Golding received a similar letter to her brother."

"It is unlikely we will find out, now."

Holmes nodded thoughtfully. "Nevertheless, it seems obvious that both deaths are connected, probably with the same motive. Doubtlessly, we shall discover more of this soon."

"It turns out then, that Miss Villiers' faithless conduct has led us in an entirely unsuspected direction." I braced myself as our carriage took a sharp corner. "My sympathies are with Mr. Janner, who has lost not only his liberty, but the woman he loves, also."

"His freedom we hope to restore soon. As for Miss Villiers, I think he is well rid of her, for she would have made an untrustworthy wife. In any case, Mr. Janner is well on the way to recovery, on that score."

I turned to him in amazement. "How can you know that, Holmes? It has been said before now that you can see deep into the human heart, but you always dismissed the assertion."

"As I do now, Watson. I was referring to something that Janner himself said in our presence. You may recall that his words were: 'I have only beaten the man who took away the woman I *loved.*' Do you see? He spoke in the past tense which indicates that, although he may not yet realise it, he has begun to forget her."

"I hope so, for it will be better for him." I glanced out of the carriage window and saw that we were leaving the city behind, as the congested streets gave way to trees and open land. "I am

18

curious about the series of low buildings hereabouts. I hear running water, so possibly they enclose bathing pools."

"Quite so," said my friend. "Those are the famed mineral springs of this area, where many claim to have been relieved of their aches and pains. It surprises me that you were unaware of them."

"I simply did not recognise them. They are not as I imagined."

By my estimation we had travelled at least three miles. Indeed, it was not long after that we found ourselves in a lane running parallel to a high continuous wall of red brick.

"We have arrived, I think," Holmes announced as tall iron gates appeared ahead.

As we came to a halt the gatekeeper, a tall, saturnine man, appeared and Holmes gave our names. The man disappeared through the gates, closing them behind him, and reappeared a few minutes later to admit us.

The four-wheeler rattled along an uneven drive lined with tall pines. We turned a corner, to be confronted by the dark shape of a crumbling house.

"I should not be surprised, Holmes, to learn that this place has remained unaltered since Cromwell's time," said I.

"Certainly it is in dire need of some repair."

Our coach came to rest on a gravel forecourt that was strewn with weeds, and at once the massive oak doors opened. A greying middle-aged man, clad in a morning-suit despite midday having passed, came out to meet us as we alighted. I heard Holmes instruct the driver to await our return.

As he approached it became evident that this man had fallen on hard times. No doubt Holmes also had noticed his frayed cuffs and his trousers that were in need of pressing. That no servant was sent to meet our arrival, added to that impression.

"Good morning to you both. I am Anthony Bersworth," he said by way of greeting.

My friend extended his hand, which was accepted. "I hope we are not disturbing you too much. I am Sherlock Holmes."

I was introduced also, and Mr. Bersworth gestured for us to precede him into the house.

"I have heard of both you gentlemen," he said. "The newspapers are often full of your commendable efforts to help the police. However, when the gatekeeper informed me of your arrival I was confounded," he smiled uncertainly, "since I have committed no crime that I know of."

Holmes appeared a little put out, to be described as a helper of the official force, but he maintained a genial expression. "I am certain that you have little to be concerned about on that score, Mr. Bersworth. We are here in connection with an unexplained death."

His face went blank for a moment, then understanding came. "You must be referring to Miss Martha Golding. But that was about a fortnight ago, and Scotland Yard informed me that the poor woman took her own life."

"There is some doubt about that, now."

We were led into a drawing-room with the dusty atmosphere of an old church. A manservant, tall and heavily built with an angry mark across his neck, appeared quietly and took our hats and coats. We politely refused Mr. Bersworth's invitation to join him in a glass of port, and settled ourselves in the old-fashioned armchairs that graced the hearth.

He appeared much shocked by the news. I noticed his hand tremble as he held his glass. "Have they found new evidence?" He asked.

"Her brother has met a similarly unfortunate end," Holmes explained, "and the two deaths may be connected."

Mr. Bersworth put down his glass and rose to clap a hand to his forehead. "Stephen? Dear God! This is too much. Are we speaking of murder?"

"I regret that it appears so. We are here to ask for your help, in apprehending the killer."

"Of course, but what can I do?"

"It would assist us greatly if you would explain your relationship with Mr. Golding and his sister."

Resuming his place in his chair, Mr. Bersworth was a picture of grief. But after a minute or two he seemed to collect himself. "If it will help, I will tell you everything from when I met them both."

"Thank you," Holmes returned. "Pray be as precise as you can."

With his grey hair falling about his face, our host began. "We first became acquainted at the Stadium Club in Pall Mall," he said in a quiet voice. "I had been a member for years and made a fair living from the cards although," he looked around the room, "I have experienced a run of bad luck lately. Stephen and his sister began attending regularly about six months ago, and at first he did well. I often conducted conversations with them between games, and we all three became close, probably because I have few friends and no relatives whatsoever. After a while Stephen began to lose too often, a run of bad luck such as I have since experienced myself, with the difference that he had not the remains of an inheritance to fall back on. I saw the effect these misfortunes were having and managed to lend them a sum, but instead of using it to live on, he gambled it away. Then they no longer came to the club, and I assumed it was because they were becoming increasingly poorer, until I heard that he had absconded with another man's bride-to-be and fled to Scotland. I was naturally shocked by this appalling behaviour and believed him to still be there, especially as he was not present at his dear sister's funeral. I cannot tell you how distressed I am to hear of his death, nevertheless."

"That is most apparent," said Holmes, and I knew by his tone that Mr. Bersworth was absolved of any suspicion. "Is it possible that Mr. Golding made any enemies at the Stadium Club? Is there anyone who comes to mind who is likely to wish him harm?"

This was not considered for long. "There was the distasteful business with Ernest Tornay, a long-standing member. Tornay is rather too inclined towards drink, as he was when he accused both Goldings of cheating one evening after he sustained some heavy losses. There was some disturbance and the threat of a scandal, but Tornay was eventually persuaded to apologise. Had he not been a member for many years I have no doubt that he would have been barred from the club, but as it was he was taken into the manager's office for a stiff lecture. I was never convinced that he had forgotten the incident, and if anyone meant the Goldings harm it would be him."

"Thank you," Holmes murmured thoughtfully. "Please describe Mr. Tornay's appearance to us."

"He is quite a large man, in fact it is rumoured that he earned his living as a pugilist during his early life. The source of his current income is not known, and I have noticed that he invariably steers the conversation away from any reference to it. His hair is thinning, but he has allowed his side-whiskers to grow as if in compensation. He is known at the club for his generosity towards the other members when he is on a winning streak, and for frequent furious exchanges at times of repeated loss. I have never seen him dressed in other than evening wear."

"My thanks to you," Holmes repeated, "for a most informative description. Doubtlessly it will aid us considerably."

"Excuse me, gentlemen."

We all turned towards the doorway, to the source of this new voice, where Mr. Bersworth's manservant sought our attention

"This is Fortescue," our host explained, "my right arm you could say. He has been with me but a short while, but, along with the cook and the maid, he runs this place. I have had to reduce my staff of late, and he is the only addition."

"Your previous manservant left your employ, then?" Holmes enquired.

Mr. Bersworth shook his head. "No, it was the strangest thing. Old Patterson had been with the estate for years, and he simply disappeared! I sent him into town to collect some cloth samples from my tailors, and he never came back. There was absolutely no trace of the man. He was quite elderly, so it seemed likely that he had been taken ill, or been the victim of an accident, but enquiries to the police, hospitals and local doctors yielded nothing."

"Most curious. What conveyance did Patterson use, to carry out the errand?"

"The dog-cart was always at his disposal for such tasks. It was brought back here later the same day by a young fellow who found the horse wandering, less than a mile away. It was then that I first became concerned."

"And no more was ever heard from him?"

"Nothing at all. The incident remains a mystery."

Holmes' frown deepened. "But eventually he was replaced to your satisfaction?"

"That happened quite quickly. Only two days later…."

"Gentlemen," Fortescue interrupted again. "I beg your pardons, but I have something of urgent significance to tell you. As I passed the door I could not help but hear your mention of Mr.

Ernest Tornay. Sirs, this gentleman is known to me, and he is watching the back of the house at this very moment."

"What!" exclaimed Mr. Bersworth. "Explain yourself, man."

"I was in the dining room near the window," Fortescue continued, "when a flash of light from the woods at the edge of the estate attracted my attention. I have keen eyesight, and was able to discern Mr. Tornay observing the house through a spyglass. He appeared to be taking a great deal of trouble to conceal himself."

"It was a rabbit-hunter, perhaps?" Our host ventured.

"No, sir! It was definitely he."

"This is outrageous! What does the fellow mean by such behaviour? I will go out there at once, to settle this!"

Mr. Bersworth's face had become red with anger. He was deeply affected, I thought, to an excessive degree.

"If I may, sir," said Fortescue, "I will recommend against that. You will recall that your physician has warned against undue excitement."

"Your blood pressure appears high," I observed from his complexion.

Mr. Bersworth passed a hand across his brow. "That is so. Any exertion tires me quickly. I live in fear of a seizure."

"Watson and I will look into this," Holmes volunteered. "Fortescue, pray show us where you saw Mr. Tornay."

All four of us went into the dining-room and stood before the tall windows that led out onto the lawn.

Fortescue pointed across the expanse of overgrown grass, to a rustic fence that was half-hidden among the trees. "You see the tall oak, sir? Just to the left of it, I saw the reflection."

"There appears to be no one there now," Holmes observed, "but he will have left traces of his visit. Come, Watson, let us see what can be learned."

"Have I your permission to continue with my duties, sir?" Fortescue asked Mr. Bersworth.

"Of course," our host replied, as he sank heavily into a chair. "Forgive me for not accompanying you gentlemen."

"I would recommend that you rest," I advised, as Holmes opened the windows.

We stepped out onto the terrace, and then onto the lawn.

"Observant fellow, that manservant," I remarked.

Holmes took my arm and guided me around the side of the house, away from our course. "Surely, you did not believe that story?" he asked.

"I saw nothing amiss with it."

"It did not strike you as an enormous coincidence that this man Tornay should appear, just as we were speaking of him? 'Passing the door'? Bah! Fortescue was listening to our conversation. He knew that we would attach especial urgency to the man's presence, and rush out after him as we are doing now. Also, how could he see the sun's reflection from a spy-glass, when the sun is wrongly positioned for it at this time of day? No, Watson, he was desperate to distract us for some reason, probably to flee, which is why we are now on our way to apprehend him."

"He is our killer, then? The murderer of Mr. Golding and his sister?"

"Perhaps. He is of the build that I expected. You will remember how much space was necessary for him to hide in Golding's wardrobe at the hotel. However, the most probable identifying factor is the gloves he wore."

By now we were coming to the end of the wall, nearing the front of the house.

"But there was nothing extraordinary about them, surely? I had assumed he had been polishing the family silver, or applying himself to a similar task."

"Yet there was not a mark to be seen. The gloves were spotless. I asked myself why else he would wear them."

"To conceal his hands from us," I concluded.

"Bravo, Watson! The stains that have undoubtedly resulted from the vitriol attack on Golding would otherwise have revealed his guilt. Yes, I believe we have discovered our murderer. I assume he attached himself to this household because of Mr. Bersworth's closeness to the Goldings, perhaps to learn of their whereabouts. But wait, I fear we are too late!"

We reached the forecourt a moment after a dog-cart sped by, driven at a frantic speed. As it passed our waiting four-wheeler it caused our horse to rear up, its front legs groping at the air. Fortescue cruelly used the whip in his haste, swaying dangerously around the corner of the drive. In an instant, he was gone from our sight. I knew that, in our heavier vehicle, we would be unlikely to overtake him.

"Our bird has flown," said Holmes. "I should have confronted him in the dining room, and not embarked on a false search of the woods. I wished to be certain, before escorting him to Hopkins."

"But his identity is now known. His capture is certain, if not imminent."

"He has shown a singular cunning in this. Consider his immediate adoption of the gloves, because he knew we would recognise the significance of the burns on his hands. No, Watson, I think Fortescue is but one of his guises, but for now we must inform Mr. Bersworth of this further distressing news."

We retraced our steps, rather than cause Mr. Bersworth to attend the front door in his disturbed state. The dining room was deserted, and I closed the windows after us before proceeding to the corridor. As we returned to the drawing-room Holmes came to a sudden halt, so that we almost collided.

I saw then the reason for his hesitation. Before us lay the body of Mr. Bersworth, his head covered in blood. Upon the carpet near him, the heavy statuette that had been used to inflict the grievous blow had been broken by the impact.

I rushed to give what aid I could, but it was a hopeless gesture. Mr. Bersworth was beyond my help, but now, it is to be hoped, he is in more merciful hands.

Chapter Four - A Visit to Pentonville

Sometime later, we found ourselves once more in Baker Street. Neither Holmes nor I had appetite, and told a surprised Mrs. Hudson that we would be content to forego a late luncheon and wait until dinner.

On our return from Great Trees Manor, Holmes had sent a telegram to Scotland Yard. It was a certainty, I thought, that Inspector Hopkins and others of the official force would be there by now and their investigation begun. Holmes had conducted his own inspection of the scene while I attempted to restore calm to the maid and cook, but he seemed eager above all to return to our rooms where he could consult his index.

I watched from an armchair while, on his hands and knees and with the smoke from his clay pipe swirling about him, he rapidly turned pages. He discarded several loose sheets and glanced up at me with an expression of frustration.

"It was here, I am sure."

"What are you searching for, Holmes?" I enquired.

He took his pipe from his mouth and gestured with it. "I am seeking a way to track down the fellow who we know as Fortescue. He is one of those criminals who rarely show themselves publicly, but others of his class may be able to find him. I have only to select the right one. After consideration, this now seems to be a more likely line of enquiry than the pursuit of Mr. Ernest Tornay."

After a few minutes he got to his feet and returned the index to its shelf.

"You have found something?" I ventured.

"I believe I have. I wonder if our friend Hopkins would be so good as to arrange for me to pay a call on an inmate of Pentonville Prison."

He quickly selected a form from a pad and scribbled a few words upon it. A moment later he had opened the window and stood looking up and down Baker Street, until he called to someone below. I heard the front door open and close, and someone quickly taking the stairs, before Billy the page knocked at our door. Holmes bid him enter and gave him the telegram, together with some coins. When he had departed we settled in our chairs and my friend put out his pipe.

"There will be no answer until early evening at the earliest," he said. "Hopkins is a busy man and we have made him more so. However, I do not think it presumptuous to say that we will be going to Pentonville in the morning."

After a dinner of Mrs. Hudson's steak and kidney pie, we spent most of the evening talking of our past adventures together. Holmes was in a rare mood where he would elaborate on certain aspects that I had not fully understood at the time, and I was able to make many notes to aid me in the preparation of future publications.

It was after breakfast the following morning when the telegram from Inspector Hopkins finally arrived. Holmes tore open the envelope and his pleased expression told me at once that it contained the news he hoped for.

"Come Watson!" he cried as he took up his hat and coat and, as an afterthought, his stick. "We have an appointment to keep."

As we boarded a hansom I heard him instruct the driver. It was indeed Pentonville that we were making for, and we were soon in an area unfamiliar to me.

"Where are we, Holmes?" I asked.

He raised his head from his chest and glanced into the street.

"This is Barnsbury, and we are approaching the Caledonian Road. The prison is quite near, now."

Shortly after, we alighted before a grim structure with metal-studded doors. Holmes rapped on them with his stick and a tiny inset panel opened to reveal an unsmiling face.

"We are here by appointment, with the permission of Scotland Yard," he said at once.

The answer, through the panel, came warily. "Your names please, gentlemen."

Holmes gave them and the doors were opened barely enough to admit us. The gatekeeper was not alone. Another officer, who was apparently our escort, requested Holmes to leave his stick behind, before bidding us curtly to follow as he turned and marched into the prison yard.

We entered the building, and found ourselves in a network of corridors that appeared more depressing even than those in Scotland Yard.

Clearly, Holmes had been here before, since he was well informed regarding the inner situation of the place.

"There are five separate wings," he whispered as we reached a central hall, "that radiate from here. The design originated in the United States of America, where it proved successful at the Eastern State Penitentiary of Philadelphia."

"This is a terrible place, Holmes."

"Indeed. Yet what else should be done, with violent criminals?" We came to an abrupt halt, mildly alarmed as a party of masked men under supervision crossed our path and disappeared into an adjoining corridor.

Our escort saw our perplexity. "They are prisoners on their way to the exercise yard," he explained. "The cloth masks cover their faces, for they are not allowed to converse."

I shuddered. "I would go mad in here."

Holmes nodded. "Many have done so. It is understandable, I think, that there are those who have pity for such souls."

"I am sure that some of them deserve it."

Our escort stopped suddenly, outside a stout door with a tiny barred window. He produced a ring with many keys and fitted one into the lock. The door swung open and he ushered us inside.

"I will remain here, gentlemen, near the door. If you need me, call out at once."

Holmes expressed his thanks and the door closed heavily behind us. I saw at once that this was not a cell but some sort of interview room. It contained only a table and three chairs, all of which were bolted to the floor. The walls were of a drab olive green and such light as there was entered through a high barred window, providing meagre illumination even with the approach of midday.

At the table sat a small grey-haired man, his hands manacled to the wall by means of handcuffs and a short chain. I would have judged him to be about fifty years of age but had the impression that he was actually younger, and that confinement had added years to his appearance.

"Good morning, Mr. Alfred Court," said Sherlock Holmes. "This is my friend and colleague, Doctor John Watson."

Mr. Court attempted to stand in greeting, but the chain prevented it. His restraints caused him to resume his seat heavily, but to my surprise he smiled.

"Good morning, gentlemen. Mr. Holmes, I never thought to see you again."

We sat in the chairs opposite, and removed our hats.

"I must apologise, Watson. I have been rather too preoccupied of late. I should have explained that Mr. Court devised a most efficient strategy that ensured the success of the Tradesmen's and Farmer's Bank robbery, some three years ago."

"I did that, sirs, but I had nothing to do with the killing of the young constable outside the building. Murder's not my game, nor ever could be, but the police were set to put a rope around my neck until Mr. Holmes proved my innocence. What I say is that five years behind bars is better than a few minutes with the hangman."

These events were unknown to me. "Was the real murderer ever brought to justice?" I asked.

"Oh yes," Mr. Court replied. "He won't be killing anybody else, not ever."

"All that was long ago brought to a successful conclusion," Holmes said impatiently. "When you regain your freedom, I hope you will seek honest work."

"Yes, indeed, sir. Yes, indeed." Mr. Court nodded with apparent enthusiasm.

I could not tell from his expression whether Holmes was convinced, but in a moment he asked a question:

"Would you be prepared to prove your repentance by helping me, Court? It is because I believe you to be one of the few men able to that I am here today."

Mr. Court smiled again. "I expected some such thing, for I cannot imagine you coming here to talk over old times with me. If I can be of assistance I will, for I feel greatly obliged to you."

"It is about Elijah Bracken, that I need information."

The prisoner, already pale from his indoor confinement, went paler still.

"You know what they call him?"

Holmes and I shook our heads, saying nothing.

Mr. Court glanced at each of us in turn, and then cringed in his chair. "'The Phantom Killer', that's what he's known as. I wouldn't cross him because he can get at you, even in here. Nobody knows how many he's killed, nor how. He does his work and slips away quietly, like a cat in the dark."

"Anything you tell us will go no further," Holmes assured him. "You must know that you can trust our word."

"Of that I have no doubt, but outside this room there stands a guard. He can hear our talk and could well pass it on in his local drinking-house. Word soon spreads."

"Very well. If you have anything to tell us then whisper, although I am quite sure that it is unnecessary."

Mr. Court said nothing, but silently looked down at the table before him. I thought I saw his body begin to tremble.

"Let me begin this by telling you something of our recent meeting with Elijah Bracken," my friend continued to encourage him. "We, and Scotland Yard, are aware that he has recently murdered a brother and sister of the name 'Golding'. We caught up with him posing as the manservant of a friend of the Goldings, whom he killed before escaping. All I require from you is the name of the place where he is likely to have fled."

Mr. Court lowered his voice. "Why do you think I would know?"

"Because you once shared a cell with him, in the Transvaal."

"How did you find out?"

"It is my business to know such things. From my records I came to realise that Fortescue, the manservant, was actually Bracken."

"You recognised the scar on his neck?"

"I did, but not soon enough. He had changed his appearance, from that published in the newspapers."

Mr. Court nodded. "He was always good at that. In South Africa he almost escaped prison by disguising himself, twice. He was there for robbing a prospector, they couldn't prove murder or he'd have hung. That was his game then though, claim-jumping. There were half a dozen other unsolved killings, and by rights they should have been laid at his door. Before the law caught up with him, he spent some time on the run, but he knew his luck was wearing thin. The way he told it to me, he forced his way into a house in one of those mining towns one night when the police were getting close. The brother and sister who lived there sound like the people you spoke of but, be that as it may, they fought him. The man threw boiling water in his face while the woman got his gun, then she went outside and screamed until the police patrol heard her."

"There, Watson, is the significance of the vitriol in Bracken's revenge." Holmes pointed out.

"Revenge," repeated Mr. Court. "He spoke of little else when we were penned up together. I think he even dreamed about it. It's no surprise to me that he killed those two. I'm just glad it wasn't me he was after."

"When did you see him last?"

"Not since South Africa. I was doing a stretch there for robbing a hotel, but they let me out early on account of my good behaviour. That always pays in prison, see? On the last morning he wished me luck when the guard came to take me out, and I've not seen him since."

"So, in fact, you cannot help us with his current whereabouts?"

"I have not said that." Mr. Court pitched his voice lower still, so that we hardly heard. "There was a place, a place he kept talking about as if it were Heaven. His aunt, the last member of his family, died and left it to him and he'd been there once or twice. He couldn't wait to get back. If he's hiding out, it's as likely to be there as anywhere."

"And where is this Earthly paradise?" Holmes enquired.

Mr. Court's body became tense as he turned his head to look at the barred window in the door. "I'm risking my life by telling you this," he said in a barely audible rush of words. "But you saved mine when all is said and done. I hope to God that nobody ever finds out I told you."

"Never from us. I have given you my word."

Again he looked nervously around him, as if he feared that some invisible listener lurked nearby.

"It was in Devon, this place. The town is called Torquay, and those who have the money go there for their health."

"And the address? Do you know it?"

"He called his aunt's home, 'King William House'."

"Thank you, Court," Holmes said appreciatively. "I will tell the prison governor, and him only, of your assistance if you permit it. It may make things easier for you."

The prisoner nodded, and stared at the floor of his cell as we left.

"What do you say to a few days in the southwest, old fellow?" My friend asked as the prison doors closed behind us, soon after.

I, of course, agreed at once.

Chapter Five - A Warning

A long train ride of alternating periods of fitful sleep and varied conversation brought us to the recently-opened Torquay Railway Station in the late evening. We gave up our tickets and carried our light bags out of the station, and at once became conscious of the warmer air blowing in from the sea. By looking down the straight avenue to our right, we could see a grey expanse of water. A good way from the shore, pinpoints of light grew brighter with the approach of darkness.

"Those are vessels of the Royal Navy," Holmes observed, anticipating my question. "The bay offers good shelter and they anchor here often."

"That fellow there appears to be waiting to meet someone with his cart."

"From his expectant attitude towards everyone emerging from the station, I should say that he is for hire."

This was soon confirmed. My friend asked that we be taken to the Prince Consort Hotel, and the man replied in a local accent that was almost incomprehensible to me. Holmes however, seemed to experience no such difficulty, and we were invited to place our bags in the cart before climbing up next to the driver. We rattled off along the coast road, turning away from the signposts to Paignton and passing numerous hotels and a long promenade as we headed into the town. Beyond the partially built Marine Spa, dark hills towered above the sea.

The cart turned to our left and the horse began a slow trudge up the steep incline of Torwood Street. The few shops gave way to a cluster of small hotels which became ever more remote from each other, and the dark silhouette of a church lay beyond a patch of lawn. Near the crest of the hill the driver drew on the reins and we were still.

"The Prince Consort, gentlemen," he said as he alighted. Our bags were unloaded and placed on the pavement, and Holmes gave the man some coins. He touched his cap in acknowledgement and left us. We watched as he turned his cart around and drove down towards the town and the sea beyond.

"I telegraphed to reserve our rooms," my friend said as we turned towards the small courtyard and the rather irregularly shaped building, "so we are expected."

The structure was four stories high, with many lights and signs of activity visible. We entered a wide reception area and gave our names, and were swiftly conducted to two Spartan but spotlessly clean rooms two floors above.

"These will do admirably," said Holmes, and asked the boy when we might dine. After changing we descended to the dining room to consume a late but passable dinner and, as we had found the journey tiring, thought it best to retire immediately afterward. Wearily, I lay on the brink of sleep for a while, listening to the distant crashing of the sea and Holmes' restless pacing in the next room. Already, I felt, he had seen dangers or difficulties ahead of us, and was grappling with them.

I met him on the stairs the next morning, and we went down to breakfast together. The dining room was well occupied, with waiters scurrying here and there amid the rattle of plates and cutlery. The smell of bacon and toast met us as we were shown to a table. We ate well, and over coffee I asked my friend how he proposed to proceed, given that we had travelled here solely on the word of a criminal.

"I do not think that Court would have played us false," he replied as he set down his cup. "His fear of Bracken was evident, but I believe there is some good in him and that he is appreciative of my previous efforts which enabled him to escape the rope."

"It is to be hoped then, that Bracken has returned here."

Holmes nodded thoughtfully. "I have not the slightest doubt that he was responsible for the sudden disappearance of Mr. Anthony Bersworth's manservant, whom he conveniently replaced. Mr. Bersworth struck me as a rather naive and trusting soul, who would have suspected nothing. King William House is our only known haunt of the so-called 'Phantom Killer' -- at least the only one told to Court, who knew Bracken well. It has occurred to me that, in a relatively small and insular society as this, Bracken may well, under a different name, be a respected member of the community. If that is so, the local force will be reluctant to act against him on our say-so, without solid proof."

"Would Scotland Yard vouch for us?"

Holmes was never to answer my question, for at that moment a waiter approached, bowing slightly as he addressed us.

"My apologies for intruding, gentlemen," he began haltingly, "but there is someone to see Mr. Sherlock Holmes." He looked first at myself and then at my friend, uncertainly.

"Has our visitor presented a card?" Holmes asked.

"No, sir."

"So you are unaware of his identity?"

"He would not give it."

"Very well. Where is he now?"

The waiter indicated the direction. "Through there, sir. He waits near the reception desk."

"My thanks to you," Holmes rose from his chair. "Come, Watson."

As we left the room I realised that it must be a man rather than a lady that awaited us, since the waiter had confirmed Holmes' assumption. I wondered if our visitor could be from the local force, contacted perhaps by Scotland Yard, until I remembered that Holmes had not divulged our destination.

The reception area at first appeared empty, until a short, shabbily dressed man emerged from the shadows near the door.

He, too, glanced at us both, uncertain as to which of us he was to deliver his message.

"I am Sherlock Holmes," my friend said at once.

The man approached, holding his hat.

"I was told to deliver this to you, sir. Into your hands, and no other."

Holmes took the envelope from him. "And who, pray, sent you on this errand?"

"I do not know, sir. I am a coachman, and a gentleman on the Esplanade approached me as I delivered a fare. Instead of boarding my hansom he gave me the envelope and told me to take it to you at the Prince Consort immediately."

"Was that all he said?"

"No, sir. He expressed much urgency about the matter, described you accurately and gave me a half-sovereign for my trouble."

"Pray describe this generous gentleman."

"There is really little to say, sir. He wore a morning suit and a top hat pulled down over his forehead. Oddly I thought, for a warm day, his face was wrapped in a thick muffler. I thought it likely that he might be suffering from influenza, and so kept my distance."

"But his build -- was he a small man, or tall?"

"Not small, Mr. Holmes. I would say as tall as yourself, but with broader shoulders."

Holmes nodded and ripped open the envelope, glanced at the single sheet it contained and handed it to me. On good quality paper was written: "*Let things lie. Leave here while you yet live.*"

"Should you encounter this man again," he told the coachman, "you may tell him that I have received such threats before, yet still I remain. Here is another half-sovereign, which you may care to use for the benefit of your infant child."

"But how could you know that, sir, about the boy?" He shrank back slightly, aghast. "Do you practice magic?"

"Hardly," Holmes smiled. "But when I see the tiredness in your face, together with the faint stain of your son's digestive difficulties on the shoulder of your coat against which you held him, I would be obtuse indeed if I did not reach that conclusion."

The coachman looked no less astonished.

"Bless you, Mr. Holmes," he said, and was gone.

#

"We know at least, that Bracken is not far away," Holmes said as we seated ourselves in his room soon after. "For how would he know of our presence or of our chosen hotel otherwise? He has local spies here and there, I dare say."

"We can be certain now, I think, that he is the manservant from Great Trees Manor, since he was able to furnish the coachman with a description of you."

"Bravo, Watson!" He exclaimed. "We are certain of our adversary indeed, as I have been since I identified him from my index."

"But how do we proceed now?"

"By making use of Mr. Court's information. This warning changes nothing."

"You still mean for us to visit his address?" I ventured after a moment.

"Exactly that. So, my dear fellow, I propose that we should collect our hats and coats and see what can be gained at King William House."

It proved more difficult here to engage a cab, since they were much less frequent than in the capital, but after strolling to the sea front we hailed a passing hansom near the Spanish Barn.

We quickly left the harbour behind, climbing an increasing incline away from the cliffs. The lanes we came upon were narrow and curved beside ploughed fields of reddish-brown earth. Tall pines stood in clusters, trembling in the sharp breeze that had sprung up. Presently, the coachman turned into a gap in a thick hedge, and we were faced with a square building of dull red brick.

Holmes instructed the coachman to wait for us and we alighted. I looked up at a rather gaunt façade, a structure that had once been elegant but was now showing signs of mild neglect. We crossed the courtyard and approached the steps leading up to a weathered door, which opened before we could knock. A butler stood before us, immaculately attired but with a severe expression such as a headmaster might reserve for an unruly pupil.

"Yes, gentleman?"

"We would like to see Mr. Elijah Bracken, if that is possible."

His frown deepened. "I know of no such person, sir."

"This address was described to us, quite specifically," Holmes persisted. "Perhaps the man of the house is acquainted with him."

"My employer sees no one without an appointment."

"Who is your employer?" I enquired.

The butler drew himself erect. "This is the house of Mr. Rodney Squires-Wilton, who is not at home to all callers, at the moment."

I turned to speak to Holmes as the door was slammed in our faces.

"Rude fellow," I observed.

"Certainly there is something that he and his master wish to keep hidden."

"Perhaps there is some other way to determine whether this man is Bracken. We could watch this house and follow the owner's carriage when it leaves. At its destination, we could accost him and compare his appearance."

Holmes laughed. "In some circumstances I would do exactly that, Watson. However, he might not leave his home for days and we would need a cab standing by constantly. No, I think there is little to do for now. By visiting his home we have thrown down the gauntlet, and if he is the man we are seeking, he cannot risk us exposing his double life."

My friend said little, except for the occasional comment on our unaccustomed surroundings, during the return journey. As we neared the centre of town he sat upright suddenly, as if a new thought had occurred to him. He rapped on the roof of the hansom with his stick.

"Driver, I have changed my mind. Pray take us to the public library."

We were there no more than a few minutes later. It proved to be a low stone building, set on a hill between a costumier's establishment and the local music hall theatre. On entering we passed a young bird-like woman who watched us disapprovingly from behind a desk, presumably the librarian. She made no offer to help, and Holmes seemed to need none, as he strolled between high shelves of leather-bound volumes to which he gave cursory examination as we passed.

"Aha!" He selected one and we took it to a nearby table and seated ourselves. "This should prove informative."

"You are looking for information about this Mr. Rodney Squires-Wilton?"

"Indeed." Holmes consulted the index and began to turn pages rapidly. "The more one knows of one's enemies, the closer one is to defeating them."

I had noticed that the volume that Holmes consulted was *Who's Who in the South West of England.* His sharp glance flitted up and down several pages until he stopped and remained perfectly still as he read.

"Look at this, Watson," He slid the book across to me.

As I expected, he had turned to the entry titled "Rodney Squires-Wilton," and it read thus:

Member of Devonshire Chamber of Commerce, Founder Member of the Sirius Club, Nominated twice as Lord Mayor of Torquay, but narrowly defeated. Unmarried, age about thirty-five but cannot be determined accurately since Mr. Squires-Wilton grew up as an adopted orphan.

"Most interesting," said I.

"You will recall my surmise that Bracken may have a different name here, even a position in local society. I notice that the entry bears no reference to his early life or his business or source of income. Undoubtedly he has a method of explaining his misdeeds away to the satisfaction of his friends and colleagues."

"What is the 'Sirius Club'? I enquired.

Holmes turned more pages. "I think the equivalent of a gentlemen's club, hereabouts. However, at this moment there is something that interests me more."

I leaned forward in my seat, curious to know what more he had gleaned.

He glanced up from the volume, his face grim. "I thought that might be the case."

"What else have you found?"

"That his parents, Mr. Albert Squires-Wilton and Mrs. Rebecca Squires-Wilton, died at the time when their adopted son came of age. A fire, the cause of which was never explained, destroyed the family home in Ellacombe."

"Could it be that their adopted son, the man we believe to be Bracken, was responsible?"

"Based on what we have experienced of him, I consider it possible."

"The man must be an absolute blackguard!"

"Given the sort of man we know him to be, I thought it likely that his murderous streak might have revealed itself at an early age."

"Evidently, he is totally ruthless," I observed.

"Indeed. We would do well, I think, to keep that in mind. You are armed, Watson?"

"I have brought my service revolver."

"Capital! It may be that we shall find ourselves in need of it soon."

"You believe then, that we are in danger, that Bracken is planning something against us here?"

Holmes remained silent as an elderly lady walked past us, searching the shelves with her eyes. After she disappeared into the next aisle, he resumed in a quiet tone.

"We have tracked him to his lair and, like all vicious creatures, he will fiercely defend it. His future security depends, in part, on him maintaining a retreat to where he can retire while the law searches for him elsewhere. Our presence here has brought this into jeopardy, and he may consider it prudent to take immediate action against us."

I nodded. "If Alfred Court is to be believed, we are opposing a formidable adversary. It would be as well to take every precaution."

"I have already begun to do that, by observing our situation carefully. Did you know, for example, that we were followed here? No, Watson, do not turn your head! In a moment I will rise and replace this volume, and then make my way back to the entrance. I will be obliged if you will take the centre aisle and meet me, looking straight ahead at all times."

We rose together. It had never occurred to me how difficult it is not to glance in one direction or another, when walking. Feeling entirely unnatural and perhaps moving a little stiffly, I directed my actions in accordance with my friend's instructions. The librarian continued to display a disapproving attitude as we left, staring down her long nose at us with a fixed scowl. We emerged into the bright early summer sunshine, exchanging no words until we reached the end of the street.

"You saw our pursuer?" Holmes asked.

"I did not look around, as you said, but I was able to notice a rough-looking fellow reading a newspaper."

He smiled. "He meant us no harm, I am sure. The same cannot be said however, of the tall grey-haired man studying *The Revised World Atlas* at a table near the corner. His manner made me think at first that the local official force is keeping an eye on our activities, but I dismissed that notion at once. Bracken alone knows why we are here, and he is unlikely to involve them. We are therefore left with the only other possibility: we are under observation by our adversary."

"That was Bracken, in there? I do not think so, Holmes. Certainly he had the height of the man we saw at Great Trees Manor, but was of much slighter build."

"Possibly it was a minor accomplice," he said, shaking his head. "But I am puzzled by the fact that he has not left the library after us. Why follow us up to a point and then cease?"

"Could he have received a signal of some kind?"

"I watched him continuously as soon as I identified his purpose."

"You are certain that he was pursuing us?"

Holmes gave me a withering look, which immediately dissolved into a smile. "Oh, quite certain," he said lightly, "I have had the experience before, once or twice."

We had walked on no more than five paces when a scream of terror halted us. Turning quickly, we saw the follower that Holmes had identified, attacking a young woman across the street. She cried out again, but Holmes was already running to her assistance.

"Look after her, Watson," he called as he ran swiftly after the attacker down a narrow alley.

He vanished into the shadows and I made to offer aid to the unfortunate woman, but a hansom swung into the street and she boarded it with such speed that I covered less than half the distance to her as the cabby whipped up the horse. I felt more than a little foolish, standing in the middle of the road helplessly as the hansom turned the corner out of my sight, but a moment later my friend reappeared with an expression that told me at once that he too had been unsuccessful.

"He was too quick for me," Holmes explained, "or his knowledge of this labyrinth saved him. Where is the woman?"

"I fear that she, too, is gone. A passing hansom plucked her from the pavement."

Holmes adopted a thoughtful look. "There is more to this. Our attention is drawn to an attack in broad daylight, on a street which leads away from the main thoroughfare. The attacker proves elusive, suggesting that his way of escape was planned in advance. Then the victim is snatched away from us when it would be normal for her to welcome our help and protection. Ha! This incident was stage-managed, Watson, like a scene from a play."

"But why? What purpose has it served?"

He strode on impatiently, with me beside him. I sensed that he was angry because he had not immediately seen through the deception that had been visited on us.

"A very simple purpose," he answered as we neared the end of the street. "The same as that of the rather-too-obvious watcher in the library, who was meant to engage my attention to delay us. When that proved insufficient, he rather theatrically attacked the young woman, who was doubtlessly waiting nearby in case she was needed. I have been blind, Watson!"

"But I still cannot understand why anyone would take such trouble to prevent our return to our hotel."

"That, I have no doubt, will soon be revealed to us," he replied as he raised his hand to summon a landau that had just delivered a fare to a house on the summit of the hill, "and I do not think the explanation will be pleasant."

On Holmes' instructions, the driver drove at break-neck speed back down into the town. We raced along The Strand, turning the heads of passers-by and narrowly escaping collisions with other vehicles several times.

We arrived at the Prince Consort and he paid off the driver who, I observed, had rather enjoyed the journey. As we entered the forecourt, I knew at once that Holmes' fears, whatever form they took, were well-founded. There seemed an unusual amount of activity in front of the hotel. Many guests who I remembered from the dining hall stood in small groups, conversing with an air of uneasiness. Three constables stood silently watching the proceedings, as a small man in a bowler hat questioned the guests.

Everyone ceased to move, as if suddenly frozen, as we approached and were noticed.

"Am I addressing Mr. Sherlock Holmes?" the man in the hat asked as he broke the stillness and stepped towards us.

"You are indeed, sir." my friend replied.

"The consulting detective?"

"The same."

We received a harsh look of disapproval, then: "I am Inspector Bowden, of the Devonshire Constabulary. There has been an… incident in the room that you are occupying."

"Pray tell us, Inspector, what has occurred."

"A murder, sir, and I must ask you some questions about it."

Holmes and I looked at each other in surprise.

"I know nothing of this," he said. "We have spent the morning in the town."

"Nevertheless, I would like an explanation of your movements. You were seen, you see, with the victim sometime earlier."

"Perhaps we could continue in the lounge, where I will tell you in detail how we have passed our time. Who was the unfortunate man?"

The inspector ran a finger along his moustache. It seemed to me, from his altered expression, to be a curious gesture of triumph. "I did not say that the victim was a man, Mr. Holmes."

"Quite so. But you did say that I was seen with the victim earlier and I have not, as yet, made the acquaintance of any ladies hereabouts. What else am I to conclude?"

"Very well," Inspector Bowden said after a moment of silence. "Let us go into the lounge."

We sat in armchairs around a small table and the inspector produced his notebook. He scribbled furiously, as Holmes related our activities since breakfast in response to his frequent questions.

"You say you called at the home of Mr. Rodney Squires-Wilton?"

"We did," Holmes confirmed.

"And were you received?"

"We were informed that the gentleman was not at home."

"Are either of you previously acquainted with him?"

"Not at all," answered Holmes, as I shook my head.

"Then may I ask as to your purpose in visiting him?"

"I sought confirmation of an event which occurred during a recent investigation."

The inspector interrupted his writing to give us a contemptuous glance. "I do not think you will find any connection there. He is highly thought of in these parts, and would never involve himself with the criminal classes."

"Possibly not. But as I'm sure you will agree, Inspector, it is always best to seek corroboration of one's facts."

Inspector Bowden ignored this. "You have stated that you visited the library, also?"

"You can easily enquire of the librarian."

"I will, sir. Be assured, I will."

"Has the method by which the victim was killed been established?" I asked.

After a long, silent look, the inspector said. "He was struck on the head with a metal ornament -- a ship's compass that adorned the wall."

The man had met a similar end to Mr. Bersworth, I noted.

"Is it known how either this man or his murderer came to be in my room?" Holmes enquired.

"Of this we are uncertain as yet, and that is one of the reasons I am asking you these questions," Inspector Bowden said rather pompously. "Some time after you say you left these premises, several of the hotel staff saw a tall man in tweeds and an ear-flapped travelling cap, such as you are wearing now, ascending the stairs with the victim. The key to the room was missing from the board in the reception area, although that is not unusual since those guests who stay here regularly are permitted to retrieve their keys when the desk is unattended."

"Did those who saw this state categorically that they recognised me?"

"If they had, Mr. Holmes, you would at this moment be on your way to the station in handcuffs. As it was, the two men were seen only from behind."

"And you have discovered no reason for this crime?"

The inspector apparently did not hear this, for no answer was forthcoming. "Do you confirm these statements, exactly?" He asked me rather sharply. "Are they an accurate account?"

"They are the absolute truth."

He grunted and leaned back in his chair, shifting his gaze from me to my friend. "We have heard of your doings, Mr. Holmes, even in these parts. I can anticipate that you will request that I allow you to examine your former room before the body is removed. Let me say from the outset that such a request would be met with a firm refusal. I will tolerate no interference in my investigation, none whatever."

"And you will have none, Inspector. I wish you well with your efforts. There is, however, one small detail that you have neglected to mention."

He eyed Holmes warily. "And what would that be?"

"The identity of the victim. Other than that it was a man, you have disclosed nothing. It can hardly be a secret, since the other guests and hotel staff already know, and it will in any case be in the local late editions."

"His name was Jonathan Durrett."

"That name is not known to me."

"He was the coachman who brought you a message as you breakfasted." He gave us both a steady look. "I take it that you gentlemen will not be leaving the county in the next few days?"

"You take it correctly," Holmes replied.

"Should you change your intentions, do not fail to notify me."

Holmes allowed a faint smile to cross his face.

"Very well, Inspector," he said simply.

The Inspector said no more, but rose and left us.

The murder room now had a constable on duty outside, and we found that Holmes' few things had been moved elsewhere.

"This is a most unexpected turn of events, Holmes," I said when we were seated in his new room.

"It is a further demonstration of our adversary's cunning and bravado. The reason for the deliberate delaying of our return now becomes obvious: it was important to allow time for the local force to examine the scene, and to be made aware of our presence here."

"Inspector Bowden seems an impudent fellow. I think he will receive a reply that will surprise him, if he telegraphs Scotland Yard that he suspects you of murder."

"Oh, he will certainly do that, Watson. He will seek to communicate his cleverness and suspicions to his superiors, as well as to glean any fact that might incriminate me."

"I would have thought that your reputation would have stood you in sufficiently good stead."

My friend lit his pipe and threw the match into the fireplace. "In London, yes, but remember that I am relatively unknown in this part of the country, despite our excursion to Dartmoor some years ago. The official force here will not welcome private intervention, any more than Scotland Yard did at the beginning of my career. You will recall the initial hostility of Lestrade and his colleagues." He saw my puzzled expression, and defined it correctly. "Of course my dear fellow, that was mostly my earlier cases, before we met and moved into Baker Street."

Shortly after, we dined on locally caught fish while uncomfortably aware of wary glances from both the staff and the other guests.

"We are watched by everyone, Holmes." I observed.

"It has been so since we entered the dining room. Do not pay them any heed, for such morbid curiosity rarely lasts."

"I was surprised that no one saw the murderer leave the hotel. His purpose, I presume, was to have you arrested, so that your investigation of him would cease."

My friend pushed away his empty plate. "Undoubtedly he wishes to be rid of us. His ruse to get the local force to do this for him has failed for now, so he will either attempt to supply them with further evidence of my 'guilt' or make efforts of his own to remove us."

"So, as we have already recognised, we are in constant danger?"

He shrugged as if this were of no importance to him. "It is hardly the first time."

I reflected on some previous instances when our situation had been similar, and wondered how many were still to come. Holmes, meanwhile, sat still in his chair, apparently distracted. This was deceptive, for I had no doubt that he had our immediate surroundings under constant observation.

"So," I said at last, attempting to make light of our situation, "we are both aware of the perils we may face. How do you intend that we should proceed?"

"Between now and when we take dinner here this evening, we must find a tailor who either sells ready-made suits or keeps a stock to rent out."

"A tailor!" I echoed.

"We can hardly attend the Sirius Club dressed as we are."

"Can we not wear the suits that we have brought with us?"

"We would appear a little shabby, I think, beside the other members."

"And you intend to meet this Rodney Squires-Wilton, on his own ground?"

He smiled, and said in a matter-of-fact tone: "It is an ideal time to confront him, Watson, don't you think?"

#

So it was that we engaged a hansom in mid-afternoon. Holmes explained our requirement to the cabby, who listened quietly before nodding and cracking his whip. The horse broke into a trot at once, and before long we found ourselves in a tiny shop beyond an arch near the further end of The Strand. The little tailor held his elderly head to one side as he estimated our sizes, rather than measured them. In a very short time, Holmes and I left carrying brown-paper parcels containing, as we had determined in the fitting-room, evening clothes that fitted us perfectly.

We returned to the Prince Consort Hotel to deposit our bundles, and it was then that I realised that my friend's mood had lightened.

"We have at least two hours, before we need to dress for dinner," he saw from his pocket-watch. "What do you say, Watson, to a ride around the suburbs of this delightful town? It will do no harm to learn a little about our surroundings, and may be to our advantage to know something of its disposition." He glanced out of the window. "A brougham has just pulled up across the road, and the departing passenger has engaged the driver in conversation. If we are quick, we may arrive there before they are finished."

With that, we hurried downstairs and out into an afternoon that had become cloudy. The passenger had turned to walk away and the driver was about to climb into his seat when we approached. Holmes engaged him, and we began a tour of the town and its surroundings. We saw many large villas of Italian design owned by, Holmes explained, rich families who sought to improve their health by enjoying the mild climate and the benefits of the various therapeutic establishments that operated within the area. Part of the Beacon Hill Headland had been dynamited in 1853, to create a tide-filled swimming pool that was known as Marine Spa. There were, I noted with approval, many open areas where residents strolled freely across expansive lawns, bordered by palm trees, pines and bay bushes. Not for the first time, my friend amazed me by sharing the knowledge that he had already accumulated.

"A refreshing change, from the streets of London, and the fog," I remarked.

"Indeed," But Holmes replied in a voice that told me he had already grown weary of our excursion, "it is not difficult to see why the town has become popular with those who have grown tired of life in the capital. I have mentioned before though, Watson, that some of the dark deeds perpetrated in these rural districts are no less criminal that those committed in the worst hovels of our city."

"The ways of humanity are much the same everywhere," I affirmed, remembering some of my experiences in foreign lands.

We left the brougham some distance from the hotel, in order to enjoy a pleasant walk. By the time we had returned and changed into our new clothes, dinner-time was almost upon us.

After our meal of rather over-cooked roast pork, we retired to the smoking room for brandy and cigars. Presently Holmes consulted his pocket watch and whispered: "It is now a few minutes before nine o'clock. I think we should go, Watson."

We left at once, ignoring the curious glances that followed us from the room. Once outside the hotel we walked at a fair pace in the direction of the harbour, hailing a hansom as it appeared from the opposite direction. That the driver was familiar with the Sirius Club was obvious, since he immediately turned the horse around and entered a network of narrow streets that ran parallel to The Strand. He brought us to a halt no more than five minutes later in a poorly lit side street of terraced houses, some of which boasted brass plates on their doors.

Holmes dismissed the hansom and we stood before the entrance. There was no sign or indication that this was the place we sought, but a dim glow emanated from beyond the glass-panelled doors. After a moment we entered, to find ourselves in a dimly-lit corridor. There were closed doors on either side, but both the light and the sound of much activity came from beyond the wide, lacquered screen ahead.

One of the side doors opened suddenly and a very large man confronted us. This occurred so speedily that I wondered whether our entering the premises had somehow set off a concealed warning device.

"Gentlemen," the newcomer began, "this is a private club, and I do not think that you are members."

"You are correct in that," Holmes confirmed, "but we are here to speak to a member who we believe may be in attendance. The gentleman we seek is Mr. Rodney Squires-Wilton."

"I do not know if Mr. Squires-Wilton is in the club tonight, but in any case our rules forbid any disturbance to our members while they are within these walls. Allow me to show you to the door."

"But surely," I interjected, "in the case of an urgent matter…"

"There are no exceptions," the doorman said, in a manner which suggested that he was tiring of this interview, "none whatsoever. While here, our members are protected completely from all distractions. That is a unique and much-valued service that this club offers."

"Not quite unique," observed Holmes, thinking, I had no doubt, of the Diogenes Club.

"Nevertheless," the man looked at us coldly and I had an impression of mounting aggression, "you must leave now."

"Very well," my friend said, "but do be sure to mention to Mr. Squires-Wilton, that we called to see him. My name is Sherlock Holmes."

He nodded. "Please come this way."

We were ushered quickly back to the entrance, and into the street.

"Ill-mannered fellow," I observed, as the door slammed behind us. "Not a very sociable club, I think."

Holmes laughed. "It is much as I expected. However, our purpose has been achieved. If you agree, I think we will walk back to the hotel, Watson, as it is a fine night. You are, I take it, armed at this moment?"

"I have my service revolver."

"Excellent. And I have brought along this stout stick."

"Are we then, in immediate danger?" I enquired as we began walking.

"You evidently did not fully understand me, earlier. Our calling at Bracken's home will be seen by him as a provocative threat. Now, in addition, he will feel pursued at his club. Surely, you see that a man who has killed so casually cannot ignore this continued risk of exposure and to the security of his retreat."

"I noticed that you ensured that we can be identified by that brute, back there."

He nodded. "I am as sure that our adversary knows of our visit by now, as I am that he was among the members behind that screen."

"So our true purpose tonight, was to warn him that we are here still?"

"I wish him to believe that we are getting closer to exposing him. In fact, I have every expectation that we will be admitted to the club tomorrow night, where we will meet Bracken, or Mr. Rodney Squires-Wilton as he chooses to call himself, face to face."

"Tomorrow is Sunday, Holmes."

"The club is open every night, according to the notice near the entrance."

"But what will you do, in order to get us in?"

"This is a provincial establishment, frequented mostly by local people, and so to gain entrance has proven difficult for a couple of strangers. But do not despair, Watson, for I intend to bring a higher power to our aid."

There were, as it happened, no incidents to delay our return to the Prince Consort Hotel that evening. Holmes went immediately to the reception area and enquired of the sleepy young man on duty whether it were possible to dispatch a telegram, at this late hour. After affirming the request, a form was produced, and on returning it completed, we were assured that a boy would be sent to the local office without delay.

"A glass of port, I think, before we retire," Holmes suggested.

I eagerly agreed, both to the port and the notion of retiring early. The air hereabouts seemed to me to have a soporific quality, although he appeared unaffected.

It was quite nine o'clock the next morning, before one of the receptionists approached our breakfast table with a reply to Holmes' telegram of the previous evening. I noticed that the man avoided our eyes as he made his delivery, and reflected with incredulity that my friend was still suspected of some connection with the murder in his room. I told myself that these were relatively unworldly folk, and that no such belief would have been entertained in the capital for long.

Not that this seemed to concern Holmes at all. "Aha!" he exclaimed as the man returned to his post. "We will have no difficulty gaining entry to the Sirius Club tonight, Watson."

"Did you somehow get Scotland Yard to reinforce our efforts?"

"Not at all, my dear fellow." He smiled as he crumpled the yellow form and stuffed it into his pocket. "I simply asked Mycroft if he could assist us. There is a loose social network connecting many of these clubs throughout the land, and I thought he could throw the weight of the Diogenes Club behind us."

"He has contacted the Sirius Club with a favourable reference or recommendation?"

"So he has stated, in his message. Tonight we will make a second attempt to enter their premises, as temporary members. I am anxious to confront Bracken, and to discover what he has made of himself here."

I nodded. "And how will we occupy ourselves until then?"

He looked across the room, through the tall windows. "I see a blue sky out there, it is another fine day. I think a relaxing walk along the beach or harbour will fill the time between now and luncheon quite pleasantly."

Despite my friend's usual aversion to exercise for its own sake, we walked down the hill and soon found ourselves in the midst of beached boats, drying nets and the smells of the sea. As it was Sunday morning, the town was almost deserted, and the sounds of singing reached our ears several times as we passed various places of worship. At one point we descended the steps from the promenade and trod on the uneven pebbles bordering the beach. I noted that the sea air seemed to have a beneficial effect on my friend, for his hawk-like features shone with health, and had even developed a little colour.

"Look out there, Holmes," I said as we faced the outgoing tide, "there seems to be something in the water."

He shaded his eyes with his hand. "Those are jellyfish which flock to this coast at certain times of year. That fellow who is walking in the shallows would do well to avoid them, since their sting can be harmful."

I cannot recall if I answered, for at that moment a great force enveloped us. A deafening noise filled our ears and clouds of sand tainted the air. Somehow I understood that Holmes was forcing me to my knees in order for us to gain the shelter of an enormous moss-covered rock that separated us from the sea wall.

"What happened, Holmes?" I asked hoarsely. My hearing was returning, but the shock of the experience felt like a weight upon me.

He wiped sand from his eyes. "Dynamite! That boulder saved us. Quickly, the steps!"

We raced, or rather staggered, across pebbles and sand to the short flight that led up to the promenade. At the top we could see nothing, save a hansom leaving the harbour and a woman and child strolling close to the Spanish Barn.

"So, the Phantom Killer has earned his name once more," Holmes observed as he leaned against the stone wall. "He is nowhere to be seen, yet cannot be far away."

"You are certain that this was deliberate?"

"It can hardly be otherwise. I think I have already mentioned that what is now called Marine Spa was carved from the rock by dynamiting, but that was completed in 1853. Also, even were that not so, work would not be in progress on Sunday. We have been fortunate, Watson, that providence was apparently watching over us. I have seldom been so close to death."

"You have not been injured, Holmes?"

He shook his head. "No, only shocked and shaken. Forgive me, old friend, for being preoccupied and not asking you the same question sooner. We are both in no fit state to continue. I suggest we engage a hansom to return us to the hotel, where a glass or two of restorative brandy will be in order before luncheon."

We were soon in one of the hotel sitting-rooms, having quickly bathed and changed our clothes, leaning back in our chairs drinking the harsh spirit. The explosion still rang in our ears, and it was not until well after luncheon that Holmes reported that for him the lingering impact had ceased. We separated in the early afternoon, and I returned to my room and dozed for a while. I was awakened by Holmes rapping urgently on my door, already changed for dinner.

We ate quickly, oblivious to the hushed remarks and furtive glances persisting from those surrounding us. Holmes' eyes glittered with anticipation of the adventure ahead, and I reflected that I had never seen him look more keenly alert.

As before, we left the hotel and made our way to the Sirius Club. The doors opened the instant my friend struck them with his stick.

A man of medium height, red-haired and resplendent in evening clothes, welcomed us with good cheer. That we were expected was obvious and I marvelled, not for the first time, at the extent and effect of Mycroft's influence. After surrendering our hats and capes we were shown into a large room with a colonnade on either side, from behind which we could hear the excited cries and sighs of high-stakes gambling. I noticed portraits of dignified men, presumably local notables, hung at intervals all around. In the centre area tables were arranged, surrounded by armchairs in which men sat alone or in the company of two or three. Many were immersed in the evening newspapers, lowering them periodically to signal one of the hovering waiters to bring refreshments. Others were deep in conversation and one man, well away from the others, sat erect and stared at nothing in particular. A party of five occupied a table about halfway down the room, and Holmes' attention was drawn immediately to them.

"There, unless I am greatly mistaken, is our manservant from Mr. Bersworth's estate."

"Fortescue?" When we had seated ourselves I stared in the direction that Holmes indicated, at a tall man who stood out in the crowd. He was undoubtedly the youngest of them and appeared to be in the midst of a serious discussion. "His build is the same, Holmes, but little else about him is similar."

"I would have expected nothing else. You will recall Alfred Court's description of Bracken's ability to transform himself."

"Are you certain?"

In the subdued light Holmes stared intently once more, and nodded after a moment. "Wait until he turns towards the gas chandelier again, and you will see the scar on his neck."

I watched closely, but was never to see it. From the direction of the entrance, the doorman of the evening before appeared suddenly. He crossed the room to the table where the man who had been Fortescue had just finished speaking, and whispered in his ear. I caught a brief glimpse of brutal features as, after receiving an answering nod, the doorman retraced his steps.

"I think the time has come to speak to him," Holmes said as Bracken's companions began to drift away.

We rose together, but remained where we were because Bracken had also got to his feet. He shook hands with the last of his companions before making his way towards us, smiling as if about to greet old friends.

I was astonished at the sight of him, and realised at once that Alfred Court had not exaggerated. Certainly, as I had remarked to Holmes, this man's build was similar. The scar also was clearly present, but the moustache, the colour and style of the hair, indeed the man's entire demeanour was unlike that of Fortescue. I became convinced that my friend was not mistaken however, when the fading acid marks on his fingers proved evident. His smile broadened as he approached, and he began with a courteous bow.

"Gentlemen, my name is Rodney Squires-Wilton. I understand that you visited my house in search of me yesterday, and attempted to meet me here in the club later. Pray tell me what it is that I can do for you."

There was a short silence, I thought while the two men appraised each other. From elsewhere in the room I heard a cry of triumph, as luck proved to be with one of the gamblers.

"I am Sherlock Holmes," my friend began as we seated ourselves, "and this is my friend and colleague, Doctor John Watson."

Mr. Squires-Wilton inclined his head and raised his eyebrows. "Of course, the consulting detective! I have often read of your admirable exploits. But what is it that brings you here? I cannot imagine how I can assist you although, of course, you are very welcome in the club."

I had expected that Holmes would immediately unmask this man as the murderer of the Goldings and of Mr. Bersworth and as the missing manservant, but he made no attempt to do so. Instead he replied courteously, after a sharp glance in my direction to ensure that I made no contradiction:

"We are in pursuit of a criminal, a man hunted by Scotland Yard who has killed many times. His name is Elijah Bracken, and we came to you after receiving information that you may have some slight connection with him. I freely admit that it is a tenuous thread we follow, but this fellow has proven so elusive that we will follow any indication, however slight."

I studied the face of the man across the table. There was no sign of recognition or embarrassment that I could see. To the contrary, his expression was exactly that of a completely innocent man, slightly confused by the nature of the question put to him.

Mr. Squires-Wilton shook his head thoughtfully. "I regret, gentlemen, that I have never made the acquaintance of such a person. I fear I cannot help you in this matter. But tell me, what was it that caused you to believe that I could have known him?"

"An anonymous letter, suggesting this, was delivered to our rooms," Holmes said before I could speak. "We have tried to trace its origin without success."

"If I saw this document, perhaps something would occur to me."

Since this was a fabrication of Holmes, I expected him to refuse or make an excuse why it could not be produced. I was surprised therefore, when he took a crumpled sheet of cheap notepaper from his pocket and handed it to our adversary.

After a cursory study, Mr. Squires-Wilton returned it to my friend. "Alas, it means nothing to me. The handwriting and the meaning are unfamiliar." He looked quickly into the middle of the room. "I regret I cannot help you and must leave you now, as there are some details that I should have mentioned to the town councillors during our earlier discussion." He rose, bowed again and made to turn away, and then hesitated. "Will you be remaining long in the town? Is there some other clue to this man's whereabouts?"

Holmes shrugged. "As I said, we are like drowning men clutching at straws. However, it may be beneficial to enjoy your fresh sea air and mild climate for a few days more, before we return to London."

"I wish you well with that, and with your journey."

When Mr. Squires-Wilton had left to seek his companions, Holmes ordered port and we sat and drank in silence for a while.

"This is a very devious enemy, Watson," he said after making sure that no one was within earshot. "He has a most convincing manner."

"Nevertheless, the scar and the marks upon his fingers identify him."

"Quite so. He knows he is at great risk, as long as we remain here."

"I had the impression that he wished to learn of the time of our departure in order to tread carefully until then."

Holmes smiled. "Oh, Watson, how you always seek the best in people! I believe that his attempt with dynamite was but the beginning, for he cannot let us leave the county to make our suspicions known to others. Make no mistake, old fellow, he will intensify his campaign against us. His pleasant disposition was but a façade. He is well aware that we know how he alters his identity. Consider: we arrive in his home territory, visit his house and enquire after him at his club before questioning him here. Does that not suggest that we have good reason, or possible evidence? No, he has to dispose of us, before we return to the capital and set Scotland Yard ablaze with his infamy."

We drained our glasses and were about to leave when a rather stout, elderly man who was clearly the worse for drink stumbled past our table.

"Good evening to you both," he began in a slurred voice, "I take it that you are friends of Mr. Squires-Wilton?"

"Not at all," Holmes replied, "we merely enjoyed a polite conversation."

"I wondered if he is still distressed, poor fellow."

"He did not appear so. Pray tell us why you are concerned."

"It has not been long, since his intended passed away suddenly."

Holmes and I glanced at each other.

"We are most sorry to hear that," I said, "but he did not speak of it."

"That is no surprise," the gentleman reflected. "He adopts a very brave face."

"What were the circumstances?" asked Holmes.

"I am Colonel Masters," our acquaintance responded as he tried to arrange his befuddled thoughts. "I sit on the town council with the others who were with Squires-Wilton tonight. He was to marry Miss Elizabeth Jervis, but she was snatched away only weeks before the wedding. The burial was the most sad that I have ever attended."

"I must express my condolences to him. Was the funeral held locally?"

"Sea Hill Cemetery is the eventual destination of everyone in this area. We keep our grief to ourselves."

67

Holmes nodded. "I am most grateful to you for this information. We were entirely unaware of the situation."

The colonel grunted something that may have been goodbye and staggered towards the entrance. It was then that I noticed that the man who had sat alone, staring and still, had drawn near and politely waited until the aisle between the tables was no longer obstructed. He wished us a curt goodnight, to which we replied, and was gone.

"Back to the hotel now, I think." Holmes said. "We can do no more tonight regarding Mr. Bracken."

"He will certainly not believe that we are remaining here to enjoy a short holiday," I said when we were once more in the street.

"Not for a moment and, as I have explained, he recognises us as a threat. We will hear from him soon, I am certain. Tomorrow we must purchase shovels and a pick, and possibly some items of workman's clothing. Apart from that, and watching for attacks on our persons, we have the day to ourselves."

Realisation dawned and I turned to him in astonishment. "Holmes! Unless I am greatly mistaken, you are thinking of body-snatching."

"Not quite, Watson," he laughed. "But, having become aware of this man's disposition, you surely cannot have imagined that Miss Elizabeth Jervis died by accident."

"Good heavens! Is there no end to this man's crimes?"

"I confess, I can see none at present."

On returning to the hotel, Holmes at once approached the night receptionist to ask if anyone had enquired for us in our absence, or if any strangers had been noticed near our rooms. On being informed that there had been no such incidents, we resolved to retire at once.

On the landing, near our doors, my friend reminded me: "Keep your door and windows locked at all times. Do not dismiss lightly the threat that hangs over us, for we do not know what shape it may take. Goodnight to you, Watson. We will meet here at eight o'clock."

With that he was gone, and I heard his door close as I entered my room. I passed a fitful night, wondering between bouts of shallow sleep what the following day had in store for us. Holmes had been right when surmising that this man Bracken had established himself in a position of authority here, while his true self was hidden from all. He would wield then, a certain amount of power among local dignitaries, magistrates and police. All advantages therefore were with him, while we had as yet no firm evidence against him. I lay pondering this but must have slept eventually for, very soon it seemed, the morning sun streamed brightly through my window.

My pocket-watch showed that I had barely half an hour to shave and ready myself to meet Holmes. He was outside my door exactly at the appointed time and wished me good morning with raised eyebrows.

"Nothing has occurred," I said in answer to his unspoken question, as we took the stairs to descend.

We experienced no difficulty in finding a table in the dining-room, and I noticed that Holmes deliberately selected one from where he could easily keep watch on the reception area and the entrance to the hotel.

"We must not delay here," he said in a low voice. "I suspect that the greater danger is outside, but I cannot be sure. Eat your breakfast quickly, Watson, and let us hope that our digestions do not suffer overmuch."

We soon engaged a hansom, after walking some distance from the hotel. Holmes instructed the driver to take us to a hardware shop, which turned out to be situated near a corner in one of the short streets further into the centre of the town. There we purchased some of the items that he had mentioned the night before. Carrying the well-wrapped tools, we found a small emporium selling workman's clothing. Despite the curious looks we attracted, since gentlemen usually have no need for such items, we made our selection and left soon after. Once in the street my friend engaged a cart that had just completed a delivery to a nearby shop, to take our parcels, suitably disguised in a large box, to the Prince Consort Hotel.

"Now we are free until this evening," he said. "We will, I think, explore this little town while remaining alert at all times. I think it best that we do not return to the hotel until it is time for dinner, so one of these delightful tea shops will provide our luncheon. Come, Watson, let us avail ourselves of some bracing sea air."

"But Holmes," I protested as we crossed from The Strand to where the harbour wall began, "you have not yet explained what we are to do tonight. From our conversation with Colonel Masters, I assume you intend for us to exhume the body of this girl, Elizabeth Jervis?" I stopped as I realised the implication of this. "Surely, this is beyond the law. I urge you to reconsider."

"Always the straight and upright fellow," he laughed. "Watson, have we not stepped outside the law before, on occasion, when this has proved necessary to accomplish a just cause?"

"More than once."

"Do you trust me, old fellow?"

"You know better than to ask."

He nodded. "What evidence do we have against the murderer Bracken, who passes himself off here as Rodney Squires-Wilton?"

"None that I can see."

"Precisely. Now tell me, supposing Bracken killed this girl, admittedly for reasons we do not yet know, by the use of arsenic or strychnine, would there be signs of this left in her body?"

I considered for a moment. "I cannot recall the colonel saying how long ago she died."

"Nor can I, for he did not. However, he did express surprise that Squires-Wilton had already recovered from the loss of his intended, and that suggests that it was recent."

"Then there would doubtlessly be traces of poison, if any had been administered."

"And you would recognise these?"

"Probably, but I am not a pathologist. We need the assistance of such a practitioner to be certain."

"Then I will find one," he said thoughtfully. "If necessary I will again enlist Mycroft's help, or that of the Yard."

"This is a gruesome business, Holmes."

"So it is, old friend, but this man must be brought to justice before more innocent souls die at his hands. You have seen that he is completely ruthless; the lives of any who obstruct his purpose mean nothing to him. But I will not insist that you undertake this distasteful task. We have until tonight for you to instruct me on the rudiments of the knowledge that I shall need to obtain our evidence."

We walked beside the sea wall, passing several unoccupied bathing huts. I looked at him astounded. "Holmes, there is no need. You surely could not think…."

"Not for a moment," he said with a new optimism in his voice. "I know my Watson."

The rest of the day was not without incident, as Holmes had warned. We had spent a little time walking in the park surrounding the Spanish Barn and emerged onto the paved thoroughfare opposite the sea wall, when a coach appeared from the direction of the railway station driven at breakneck speed. Holmes, as usual, was quicker than I, and swept us both back and into a flower bed as the horses missed us by inches. We regained our balance and straightened our clothes, watching the coach disappear into the town while the few people walking nearby looked on in astonishment.

"His first attempt today, Watson." He said, a little breathlessly.

"Were it not for your quick action he would have succeeded. Thank you, old fellow."

Holmes nodded in acknowledgement. "But make no mistake, we have not seen the last of him."

"The driver wore a hat pulled low on his head, and a muffler wrapped around his face."

"As I noticed. Such protection is unnecessary at this time of year, but of course he sought to conceal himself."

"You do not doubt that it was Bracken, then? It could not have been a simple case of a driver losing control?"

"I believe that coincidence, if it exists at all, is far rarer than most of us accept." We began to walk back towards the harbour. "But I recall a rather quaint little shop displaying what appeared to be an excellent menu, just beyond those small boats that are suspended in dry dock. I suggest that we repair to that establishment and fortify ourselves, before continuing our explorations."

We consumed two fine steak-and-kidney pies, before setting off along the promenade in the other direction. The road became a steep hill edged by the sea wall, and we looked down at the incoming tide as it swirled into foam around the jagged rock pinnacles that, I imagined, had brought many craft to grief. I remarked on the subject to my friend.

"There have been many shipwrecks here over the centuries, it is true," he recalled. "I remember reading of the *Nuestra Senora del Rosario*, which was among the ships of the armada in 1588. Blown from its intended destination, Plymouth, by a severe storm, it foundered on the rocks in the bay. Many of the crew were taken prisoner and incarcerated in the barn near Torre Abbey, where we strolled this morning. So it was that the structure became known as 'The Spanish Barn'."

"Really, Holmes," I said, watching a particularly high wave as it was rent asunder, "there is rarely a dull moment with you."

He did not reply, but became very still. A moment later he shaded his eyes with his hand and peered into the distance.

He had been silent for several minutes, before I asked: "What is it that has arrested your attention out there?"

"We are being observed."

"By Bracken?"

"That is most likely. I became aware of the sun reflecting from one of the boats at anchor on the other side of the bay. I believe that he is watching us through a spyglass."

I stared in the direction he indicated. "It would appear so, unless the reflection is from the boat's metal fittings."

"I can see, vaguely, the shape of the man holding the glass. The distance is too great for me to recognise him."

"Holmes, is he alone in this?"

"I think it most likely, except for casual hirelings such as he used at the library, and probably elsewhere. They will know nothing of him or his activities, their function is to obey his instructions and ask no questions in order to obtain payment for their services. Remember that it is of the utmost importance to him to keep the true nature of his activities secret from his friends and colleagues here. This is his place of refuge, his sanctuary between his unlawful escapades. To involve another in his attempts to be rid of us would require an explanation and the sharing of things he would much rather keep to himself."

"So he, himself, drove the coach that narrowly missed us earlier, and it is he that now observes us from the sea?"

"While formulating his next attack, I have no doubt. I suggest that we continue to the summit of this hill and then retrace our steps, unless there is another way back to the harbour."

"We should report this man's behaviour, before he has more success."

"Report him to whom, Watson? I could not imagine we would be easily believed by the likes of Inspector Bowden. You saw his disapproval of me at the hotel. My word against that of the locally respected Rodney Squires-Wilton will bear little weight, I think."

I nodded. "And we have no real evidence."

"As we have concluded."

"If we step smartly, we may reach the hotel before he can return from the bay."

"Perhaps, but do not let down your guard for a moment."

Chapter Nine - Miss Elizabeth Jervis

We returned to the harbour without incident, and had actually begun the long climb up the hill of Torwood Street when Bracken made his final attempt.

About half the distance was behind us when Holmes stiffened like a terrier, in the way that he had when something suddenly arrested his attention.

"Over this wall, Watson! Quickly, if you wish to preserve your life!"

His tone was so urgent that I did not think to question the order. Almost at the same instant we leapt up and over the low brick wall and into the garden of a roadside cottage.

We landed between two fragrant flower beds and crouched low, as the uppermost row of bricks exploded. For several moments we held our position, with our eyes watering in a cloud of brick dust. By the time we were able to look over the wall, it was to see a cart that had rushed past us in a surge of speed, racing down the hill.

"Another close call," Holmes said. "I wonder if anything unpleasant awaits us at the hotel."

"Bracken has been busy today," I observed.

"The fellow is becoming a little tiresome, I think. Perhaps tonight will provide some concrete facts to enlist the official force on our side." He examined the fractured bricks. "A shotgun of impressive bore, I have no doubt."

"This time he presented himself in the guise of a carter," I reflected.

Holmes nodded. "He grows more desperate."

On entering the hotel Holmes again asked if there had been any enquiries for us, and was answered that there had been none. We dressed for dinner and met on the landing. At his suggestion we first sat at a table in the lounge and consumed a brandy each, although I had no doubt that the real purpose of this was for him to observe once again the hotel entrance and our fellow guests.

As we ate I noticed that the interests of the others in us had faded. There were now far fewer curious or suspicious glances, which I attributed to the fact that a good proportion of guests who were present at the time of the murder had now left the hotel. Most of the remainder, some of whom had been questioned by Inspector Bowden, appeared to have lost interest.

"It is now too long ago to be an interesting subject for conversation." Holmes remarked as he finished his soup.

"So it would seem," I responded, before suddenly realising that I had explored the matter only in my thoughts.

"My dear Holmes!"

"No, Watson, I cannot read your mind. I can, however, sometimes define your thoughts with some accuracy from your expressions and movements. You have known me to do this before now."

"Indeed, I have. Sometimes I feel that you amuse yourself at my expense."

"Not so," he adopted a mildly outraged expression, "but when I see you peering from table to table as you eat, as well as looking a little relieved as you do this, what else am I to conclude in the circumstances?"

The main course of roast duck arrived at that moment, and we ate heartily. The conversation resumed in another direction shortly afterwards.

Holmes paid scant attention to the fruit-and-custard pudding that followed, but I attacked it enthusiastically. We both enjoyed a cup of strong coffee afterwards, and I could not help but notice the exaggerated slowness with which he conducted himself.

"You are in no hurry tonight, Holmes."

"You observe correctly, Watson. I am ensuring, from this excellent vantage point, that Bracken is not nearby. As he is quite expert in the art of disguise, he will be difficult to recognise."

I nodded. "As we have seen already today. Is it not less likely though, that he will make further assaults against us so late in the day? He seems to spend his evenings at the Sirius Club and possibly other places with local dignitaries, and we have established that he usually attacks alone."

"I considered our reasoning sound on that score, but we cannot be *absolutely* certain. If we take into account the ruthlessness that this man has demonstrated, and his apparent arrogance, then we must conclude that our best course is to proceed with every caution." He reached into his waistcoat and consulted his pocket-watch briefly. "But now I see that the time for us to act is drawing close. The reflections in the windows tell me that the street lamps have been lit and it will certainly be fully dark within the hour." He got to his feet. "Come, Watson, we will repair to our rooms."

On the way we passed through the lounge where, as before, many of the guests were taking their ease. Holmes came to a sudden halt and I saw his expression change to one of grim purpose. As we took the stairs I asked him what he had seen.

"Did you not see the headline of the newspaper on the table next to the two unoccupied armchairs?" he answered.

"I confess that I did not."

"It illustrated our dangerous position very well. The article was concerned with a find, earlier in the day, of the body of a local man who earned his living delivering vegetables from the outlying farms. He had been brutally slain, and his horse and cart were nowhere to be found."

"Good heavens! Did this occur nearby?"

"Quite near. He was found in Higher Lincombe Road."

"Then it could have been Bracken?"

"I am certain of it. It was the cart he used for the shooting. No doubt it will soon be found abandoned."

"This man is a danger to everyone."

"That becomes more evident by the hour. But we have a night's work ahead of us that may prove useful in exposing him. Let us delay no further."

We separated and met again shortly afterwards, wearing the workman's clothing that we had purchased for the purpose.

"I had considered that we should both adopt a disguise," Holmes said as we turned into a narrow passage that I had not seen before, "but if we leave by the rear entrance we are not likely to be seen. The use of this corridor at this time of day is infrequent."

It was, I reflected, typical of my friend to have prepared for our concealed departure in this way. He would have taken note of the comings and goings along our intended path in advance. That he rarely left anything to chance, I knew well.

Carrying our tools, we made our way to The Strand. We had some difficulty, no doubt because of our appearance, in engaging a hansom. When we finally achieved this, Holmes gave the driver instructions for a destination some distance from Sea Hill Cemetery. In addition, he was careful to engage me in conversation during the journey. This was for the driver's ears and to the effect that we were returning home from a day's work in another part of the town.

"I felt it wise to give the cabby some sort of explanation," he said as we watched the hansom's lights fade into the darkness. "Otherwise he might have concluded that two rough-looking men with shovels and a pick embarking on a journey at this time of evening could be up to no good."

I nodded. "He might have reported the encounter to the local force?"

"Precisely. If luck is against us, he could meet a constable by chance along the road and mention that he took a couple of ruffians to the vicinity of the nearby graveyard. There was nothing I could do against such a possibility, save give him a destination that is some little distance from our true one."

"Nevertheless, it is not far."

"If the hotel map is to be trusted, the gates are around the next corner."

He was proved correct. A short street of three-story red brick villas ended in tall iron gates. Few of these houses showed any light, and the only sound was the howling of a dog some way off.

We approached the gates and peered through the bars. The street lamps penetrated the darkness sufficiently for us to make out stone angels and crosses, and the occasional pillared family vault. Everything was still and silence hung heavily in the air. We had little difficulty in climbing the wall, since the bars of the gate provided a good beginning to our ascent. I watched as Holmes dropped to the ground onto a gravel path, and quickly followed.

I must confess to some misgivings as we made our way along the aisles between long rows of graves. I have never considered myself a particularly nervous or imaginative man, but such close proximity to the dead caused me to look over my shoulder every few yards and my skin to crawl. Holmes however, seemed to suffer no such effects. He strode purposefully ahead, periodically examining likely gravestones in the light of his dark lantern.

"How do you know where to look, Holmes?" I whispered.

"I am trying to find the newest graves, by the condition of the headstones and the newly turned earth. The most recent burials seem to be to our left, in the corner near that large oak."

It was hard to make out where my friend indicated, but slowly we progressed to the far edge of the cemetery. As we searched there was no change to our surroundings, except that a light summer mist appeared and swirled around some of the statues. An owl hooted from somewhere close, startling me, but Holmes was unperturbed. He came to a sudden halt and turned to me, so that the flickering light lit up his features.

"Here it is, Watson! He cried triumphantly. "Now, a little digging may reveal much."

We said no more, but laid down our workman's coats and took up our shovels. I plunged mine into the loose earth, and Holmes was poised to do the same, when we became aware that something around us had changed. Then came a movement from behind the trunk of the oak and a figure appeared from the shadows.

"Good evening, Mr. Sherlock Holmes. It would be a waste of your time to continue, I assure you, since all you will discover is a coffin filled with bricks."

We were still at once, watching in surprise as the moon emerged from the clouds and a silhouette became distinct. He was a tall man, as tall as Holmes, and in the glow from a lamp in the street beyond I saw that he wore a top hat and evening clothes. As he drew nearer, I could make out a face that I had seen before, and recognised him as the man who had sat alone in the Sirius Club.

"Do not be alarmed gentlemen, I mean you no harm. There are things I must tell you, if you will be sworn to secrecy as men of honour."

"You know us, then?" Holmes enquired, his voice steady.

"More accurately, I know *of* you. A young fellow of my acquaintance once had dealings with you, and related them to me with approval."

"May I ask his name?"

The newcomer came to a halt. "Mr. Hall Pycroft."

"The stockbroker," I remembered. "I wrote an account of the affair."

"Indeed you did, Watson," my friend commented wryly, "with your usual excess of drama." He moved to face the man squarely. "And you sir, who are you and how is it that you come to be here?"

For the first time, I saw a faint smile appear on the man's pale face. "You will recall, I am sure, our brief encounter at the Sirius Club. I chanced to hear your exchange with Colonel Masters shortly before he left. This presented no difficulty, as I am blessed with what a physician has been pleased to describe as abnormally acute hearing. I noted that you asked the colonel about the burial place of Elizabeth Jervis and, knowing your reputation, immediately saw the possibility that you would attend here with the intention of securing some form of evidence against Rodney Squires-Wilton."

"I commend you on your powers of foresight and reason," Holmes said.

"My thanks to you, sir. I left the club straight afterwards to come here, in case you decided to act immediately, and returned tonight. I had resolved to do likewise for the next few nights, or until I was satisfied that, after all, you had no such intention."

"But what is your purpose in this?" I asked.

"My name will explain all to you. I am Vincent Jervis, the father of Elizabeth Jervis, the former fiancée of Rodney Squires-Wilton."

"Who, as you have stated, does not lie here," Holmes recalled.

"Indeed she does not. But it was imperative that Squires-Wilton should believe so."

"How did this come about?"

"I conspired with our physician, Doctor Howard, to have my daughter pronounced dead. The burial was effected with ease, since I am the local undertaker. The good doctor has since died of natural causes, so the secret has been mine alone until now."

"Your daughter still lives!" I retorted.

"The deception was necessary to prevent a further attempt on her life by Mr. Squires-Wilton," Holmes anticipated. "Is that not so, sir?"

"It is," Mr. Jervis acquiesced. "He attempted to end her life, and would do so again if he knew of her survival."

"But could you have not enlisted the help of the police?" I protested.

"I would not have been believed. Squires-Wilton is too powerful in this town, with many influential friends. There have been rumours of his previous dark deeds, but no case has ever reached the courts."

Holmes extinguished his dark lantern. "It will be small comfort to you, but we are of the same mind."

"Then my conclusion that you are here to expose him was correct?"

"I will not deny it."

"Then can I prevail upon you to accompany me to my home? An interview with my daughter may prove illuminating to you."

"Most certainly," Holmes took our shovels and the pick and concealed them among the long grass near the oak.

Mr. Jervis seemed relieved. "I have a four-wheeler waiting, if you will come this way."

We followed him along a gravel path to the far side of the cemetery. Near a tiny chapel stood iron gates, of the same appearance as those by which we entered, which we passed through with the aid of a key produced by our guide.

The road in which we now found ourselves was bordered by a few scattered houses and open fields. A chill wind had arisen, and the horses stamped their feet impatiently as we boarded the carriage. The silent driver seemed to need no instruction, and shook the reins to bring the horses to a trot. We did not pass through the town centre, but eventually entered a district the name of which was hidden by branches that overhung the road sign. During the journey, Mr. Jervis spoke only once, in a guarded whisper:

"Pray refrain from any mention of our business, gentlemen." He pointed to the front of the coach, above where the driver sat. "Jenkins is not privy to any of this."

Holmes and I nodded silently, and nothing more was said until we came to rest before a villa that, in the dark, seemed vaguely reminiscent of the Italian style. It was a high building, boasting several towers and set back from the road.

"You may sleep in the coach or go home," Mr. Jervis said to Jenkins, "but if you leave, be sure to return in two hours."

The coach rattled off into the darkness, and we followed our host into the house. We entered a comfortable living-room and he turned up the gas-mantle as we stood before a roaring fire that dispelled the chill of the night. Mr. Jervis removed his hat, and the strain in his face was evident. He summoned no servant, but himself relieved us of our hats and coats.

"I will ask my daughter to join us," he said as he left the room.

Several minutes later he returned, accompanied by a tall girl with long auburn hair. Mr. Jervis introduced us.

"I must apologise for our appearance," Holmes began, referring to our rather soiled workman's clothes.

"I am aware of the situation," she said in a strangled croak that startled us. "But it is I who must apologise for the way I must sound to you gentlemen," she paused and I saw that she was fighting back tears, "but it was not always so."

"Come," Mr. Jervis said to us, "let us make ourselves comfortable. Elizabeth will tell you all, so that you may know the extent of the black deeds of the man you seek."

With that we settled ourselves in the armchairs near the fire, and our host served glasses of a fine brandy. Miss Elizabeth kept her eyes downcast, and rarely spoke unless addressed or questioned by her father.

Mr. Jervis spent some time in telling us of Rodney Squires-Wilton's rapid rise in the town, since his return from travels abroad some years earlier. He described how our adversary had gained the confidence of many Town Council members and others of influence. In particular, he mentioned that many minor transgressions had been ignored by the local force.

"So you see, gentlemen," he concluded, "the difficulty that you face. Within this area Squires-Wilton is considered almost beyond reproach. I have brought you here to listen to my daughter's account, in the hope that it may assist you."

"Pray continue," Holmes said in an encouraging tone.

Miss Elizabeth struggled to speak with obvious difficulty, and her father put his arm around her shoulders.

"Her confidence has been crushed. She finds it hard to relate her experience to strangers, but if we are patient she will summon the will to tell us."

"Miss Elizabeth," I said to the girl, "you are among friends here. We seek to destroy the man responsible for your condition, for the sake of his victims and those he may ruin in the future. If we cannot help you, then at least we can ensure that he does no more harm."

A few moments passed, I thought while she gathered her thoughts or summoned some courage. She finally spoke in a strained and painful voice.

"Thank you, doctor, for such kind words. My father has faith that you and Mr. Holmes can deal with this man, and I can only applaud that. I will tell you from the beginning, of my association with him."

She paused, and drank from a water-glass. Then, with an apparent effort of will, she raised her head and faced us.

"I had heard rumours about Rodney Squires-Wilton, long before he began his pursuit of me," she began with some embarrassment. "He did so relentlessly, so that I was hard put to raise any resistance. My father, at that time, knew nothing to contradict the honourable standing that this man has here, and so could not warn me. In time I told myself that I had begun to care for him, though now I cannot believe that I could have been so deluded, and our courtship intensified. The arrangements were made and the date of the wedding set, and somehow I brushed my doubts aside in the turmoil of it all."

A burning log fell into the grate, and Mr. Jervis used a fire-iron to replace it. I saw that Holmes' interest was aroused, and his eyes glittered with anticipation.

"Three weeks before we were due to be wed," Miss Elizabeth continued, "he took me to his home, King William House. We were to have tea, but had hardly begun when a visitor arrived. I did not see the man, for Mr. Squires-Wilton conversed with him in the entrance hall, outside the living-room where I remained. The door had been left slightly ajar, I cannot think but accidentally, and I was able to hear most of what was said. I tell you, gentlemen, that I could not believe my ears. Murder was discussed and there were references to other crimes, and after a few minutes I began to believe that I was living in a nightmare! I forced myself to concentrate while appearing to examine the elaborate embroidery that covered the chairs, and it soon became apparent that the man I was about to marry was not the man I thought I knew."

"It seems rather careless," Holmes mused, "for him to allow you to hear such a conversation."

"The room is quite a large one, but I am blessed as my father is, with keen hearing. I believe it was thought that I was out of earshot." She glanced quickly at Mr. Jervis. "I told my father of course, and no one else, but somehow my husband-to-be became suspicious. It was shortly after that he attempted to poison me."

"How did that come about?"

She closed her eyes for a few seconds, as if flinching from the memory of her suffering.

"Two or three day later we, my father and I, received an invitation to dinner at King William House. In view of the things I now knew of him, I had been attempting to summon the courage to tell Rodney that our engagement was over and that I wanted nothing more to do with him. Therefore, I was hesitant about accepting the invitation, but my father insisted that it was the ideal opportunity to confront him with the news and thus to sever every connection."

"And so we attended, to my everlasting regret," murmured Mr. Jervis.

"We were welcomed with excessive warmth and joviality," Miss Jervis remembered, "and in retrospect, knowing Rodney's usual disposition, I should have been warned. All went well during the meal, and Rodney made no mention of our forthcoming marriage, but there was something about the way he looked at me when he thought I was unaware of it that put me on edge. He had served a very dry dinner wine which left a harsh taste on the tongue, making a special effort to have my glass refilled several times more than I would have liked. By the time dessert had been consumed my glass had remained untouched for some little time, but a burning began in my throat that caused me to cry out. I found that I could not get to my feet unaided and my stomach was on fire. I remember nothing else of that evening, but apparently Doctor Howard was called."

"I was able to meet him in the courtyard," Mr. Jervis said, taking up the story, "before Squires-Wilton got near. I have seen enough of the dead in my profession to know them from the living, and I knew that for my Elizabeth there was still hope. In a few whispered words I advised my old friend of the situation as I saw it, and he agreed to keep the secret from Squires-Wilton, about whom he was reluctant to believe such a murderous act. After being pronounced dead, Elizabeth was swiftly carried to the doctor's brougham and transported back to his surgery. I accompanied them after feigning excessive grief, and Squires-Wilton expressed his condolences as we left. Later, I wondered why only Elizabeth was affected, and came to the conclusion that the glass that she drank from had been somehow prepared."

"I must congratulate you again, on a demonstration of uncommon presence of mind."

"Thank you, Mr. Holmes. My actions were governed by desperation. I had no means of knowing how long Elizabeth would survive without medical assistance."

"She would not have, even for that short time, had arsenic or strychnine been administered," I commented.

Mr. Jervis shook his head sadly. "This was Doctor Howard's fear also. As we rode in the brougham he tried to prepare me for the worst, but after tests he determined that neither of those poisons were present. He concluded that a natural substance had been used, a vegetable poison. Fortunately, he had seen similar effects during his travels in Africa, years ago, after the application of the ground root of a plant commonly found there. He treated Elizabeth with a mixture of several compounds, dissolved in a great deal of milk, and we knew within the next two days that her life had been saved. The remaining effect you have heard in her voice, and there are occasional fainting spells."

I saw that Miss Elizabeth's cheeks were flushed with the memory of the discomfort and the events.

"I can recall nothing more," she said, "until I awoke in bed at Doctor Howard's house. He and my father nursed me back to health, and were the only ones who knew that I still lived. The funeral was organised, and a suitably weighted coffin buried. I cannot tell you, gentlemen, how strange it is to know that, while you sit hidden at home, everyone believes that you are being lowered into the earth less than two miles away."

"Extremely distressing, I am sure," Holmes agreed.

"An extraordinary situation," said I.

"Indeed," she acknowledged, "but preferable to the alternative."

"As I have indicated," Mr. Jervis said in a tired voice, "Doctor Howard is now deceased. That Elizabeth still lives is not known therefore, outside of this room."

"Was there anything unusual about his death?" Holmes asked.

"I see the direction you are taking, Mr. Holmes, but it is unlikely. He died in his bed, or rather a bed in a hotel, while taking a short holiday in Wales."

"While Squires-Wilton was seen to be still in Torquay?"

"From time to time, he acts as an advisor to the Town Council on various matters. I believe there was a meeting on the very day of Doctor Howard's death."

"And you are quite sure that he has no suspicion as to Miss Elizabeth's survival or of your knowledge of his attempt to poison her?"

"Had he the slightest inkling, he would not have failed to act upon it, before now."

"That seems certain. Watson, I think we have reached this man's limits at last."

"I never wish to meet anyone more evil, Holmes."

"It rather seems as if our Phantom Killer has finally taken on substance," he said.

The conversation continued for almost two hours. It had served to make Holmes and myself doubly aware of the depths to which our foe was prepared to sink, and we could not help but feel that he took a mocking pleasure in the cloak of respectability which concealed him.

A short silence descended upon us, and Mr. Jervis held his head to one side.

"I hear Jenkins returning, with the four-wheeler."

"Then we will bid you both goodnight," Holmes said as we rose, "or rather, good morning. Be assured that we will do everything within our power to bring this man to justice, however long it may take."

We said our farewells and began the journey back to the Prince Consort Hotel, during which we hardly exchanged a word. On arrival we discovered that the rear entrance was locked, but with the aid of Holmes' pick-lock we quickly gained entry. After he re-fastened the door we made our way stealthily to our rooms, but as we passed through the reception area I saw to my surprise that the young man at the desk awaited us.

He regarded us bleary-eyed, apparently without noticing our unusual appearance.

"Good morning, gentlemen. I am sorry to say that your visitor has left, Mr. Holmes. He saw that your key was not on the board and went up to your room. After knocking several times he could get no answer."

"Doctor Watson and I left by the rear entrance to take an evening walk in your delightfully mild climate," Holmes replied in an even tone. "We were surprised to meet some old friends who invited us to their house. I am afraid their hospitality caused us to stay longer than we intended. Did my visitor leave his name?"

The young man, who still appeared barely awake, shook his head.

"No, sir, but Inspector Bowden is known to everyone here."

We thanked him and ascended the stairs.

"Had it been anyone else looking for us, I would have searched our rooms thoroughly to ensure that he had not left something harmful," my friend remarked. "But as it is, Watson, I will wish you a pleasant rest, in such time as remains before breakfast."

With that, we retired to our rooms.

#

Inspector Bowden arrived as we left the dining-room, after breakfast next morning. Holmes and I were at the foot of the stairs, when my friend's sharp eyes saw the official detective about to ask for us in the reception area.

"Good morning, Inspector," Holmes said in his most jovial manner as we approached. "I hear that you visited us previously. Unfortunately, we were out for an evening stroll."

Our greeting was returned, and we moved away from the passing parade of guests, into a quiet corner. That Holmes did not intend to prolong the conversation was evident to me, since he made no move towards the armchairs in the lounge.

"I did indeed mean to seek you out," Inspector Bowden responded. I came to tell you that we have found no evidence which might indicate the murderer of Mr. Jonathan Durrett."

"I am truly sorry to hear that."

"And," the Inspector looked faintly embarrassed, "it occurred to me that I might have left you with the impression that you were suspected."

"I thought you had considered the possibility."

"Not to any extent. I should mention that you have now no reason to delay your return to London, if that is your intention."

"No doubt we shall do that in the near future," my friend said without a trace of recognition of the ill-concealed recommendation, "as soon as our business here is concluded."

"I recall that you stated previously that your 'business', as you refer to it, concerns Mr. Squires-Wilton."

"That is so."

"Did you bring it to a successful conclusion?"

"Let us say that we learned much from our meeting with him."

"In that case there is nothing to keep you here. I have mentioned before that we need no outside help to solve our local crimes."

"And I have offered you none, until now. I will tell you the name of the murderer of Mr. Durrett, and that I am close to proving my case."

The Inspector, I noticed, held his hat at his side, gripping it tightly.

"Are you again referring to Mr. Squires-Wilton?"

"The same."

"Then I should remind you both of the laws of slander. I shall certainly make Mr. Squires-Wilton aware of your accusations, when he returns from the capital."

"You are better informed that I, Inspector. I had thought him to be still in town."

"He left this morning, on the early train. Many of us here would be glad if you would do likewise."

The Inspector turned and left without another word.

"Not a likeable fellow," I remarked as we ascended the stairs.

"Quite so, but he did convey some interesting information," Holmes said.

"I thought he said very little of any use."

"Not even the fact that our adversary has changed his hunting-ground?"

"That means we are safe from him here, surely?"

"As far as we know. But mark my words, Watson, we will be anything but safe, from the moment we set foot in London. He knows we must return there, and that we will do so immediately when we learn that there is no further reason for us to remain here. The other significant point of course, was the Inspector's disclosure that the official force has made no progress in their investigation of the coachman's murder."

"How is that significant?"

We came to a halt on the landing, near our rooms.

"It serves as confirmation: they have found no culprit because there is none -- other than we have already indicated to the Inspector. When he realises that he has no possibilities left, he will consider what I have suggested. Perhaps when a few things fall into place, he will not dismiss us so readily."

"But you believe that we will have solved the case by then?" I ventured, reading his expression.

"I consider it more than likely."

"Then how do we advance now?"

"By doing exactly as Bracken expects. After returning to our rooms and packing our things, we will settle our accounts and leave the hotel. I seem to recall that there is a train just after midday."

He was correct in this. Our return to the capital was uneventful, except for one incident. The train was a slow one, calling at nearly every station. As we drew into a provincial halt, a tiny place where farmers and pigeon-fanciers made up most of the waiting passengers, I saw that Holmes, who sat opposite me, had suddenly concentrated his attention on something that he had noticed on the platform.

He turned away from the window and glanced through the connecting door to the next coach.

"You have your revolver, Watson?"

"It is in my pocket."

"You would do well to keep it by you."

He said no more, but maintained his alertness until the train was once more in motion, when his features relaxed.

"What did you see, Holmes?" I enquired.

"I saw an attempt on our lives foiled by circumstance."

"Whatever do you mean, old fellow?"

"Did you not notice the small party of workmen, waiting on the platform?"

"Of course. I imagine they will board the next train."

"Doubtless, but I observed that one, standing apart from the others, was about to join us here until he noticed the contingent of Scots Guards, who have since settled in the next compartment for their journey north."

"You believe that this was Bracken?"

"I am sure of it. His disguise, the workman's clothes and the red wig, were quite well adopted, but I caught a glimpse of the scar on his neck."

"Good heavens! Clearly, he never intended for us to reach London."

"Another example, perhaps, of his criminal cunning. He expected us to be off-guard during the journey, because we were told that he had gone on ahead. I have little doubt that he conveyed to Inspector Bowden a veiled and subtle suggestion about his departure without the Inspector realising that he had been primed, so to speak, to disclose it to us. Bracken would have expected us to take the first available train, or one soon after, to pursue him."

"And he waited at that station, watching the windows of the London trains, with the intention of boarding ours when he saw us?"

"Precisely." Holmes took out his pipe and lit it.

"So that he could murder us during the journey?"

"By one method or another. As I said, the presence of the military hereabouts probably dissuaded him."

Early evening had arrived, by the time we found ourselves trudging up the stairs to our rooms. We had no sooner unpacked our bags when Mrs. Hudson presented herself, serving us with some excellent boiled ham. When she had cleared away our plates we retired to our armchairs and Holmes poured us each a glass of brandy.

"I am glad to find no unpleasant surprises awaiting us here," I remarked as he resumed his seat.

"You are thinking of Bracken?"

I nodded. "It occurred to me that he might have devised some way of anticipating our return."

"It occurred to me also, knowing as we do the depth of his ruthlessness. But what causes you to believe that he has not done this?"

"We have seen no sign of...," I looked cautiously around the room, "anything to suggest that he has, surely?"

Holmes" eyes twinkled with amusement. "There is at least one possibility."

"My dear fellow, what have I missed?"

"Nothing more than the accumulated pile of letters that arrived during our absence, which our good lady has placed upon the desk. Most of them are doubtlessly bills, but there may be some that present new problems. I am particularly interested in that large packet, bound with string and brown paper."

Feeling a little uneasy, I looked where he had indicated. "Do you suspect that it contains something dangerous?"

"I really would not let your imagination overtake you, Watson, as you do when recounting our experiences for your reading public. The package is unlikely to contain anything alive, since it is at the bottom of the pile and has therefore been there the longest, and it has insufficient bulk for the contents to be anything in the nature of an explosive device. Nevertheless," he rose and walked across the room to the desk," I shall exercise caution as I open it."

With that he proceeded to extract the packet from beneath the pile of envelopes and, holding it at arm's length, to turn it over carefully. For fully five minutes he handled it as if it were made of the finest gossamer, before holding it up to his ear and listening.

"Nothing," he announced. "Precautions were probably unnecessary."

He then startled me by dropping it back onto the desk while listening to the impact, then by throwing caution to the winds by cutting the string and removing the brown paper with no special care.

"A flat cardboard box," I observed.

Holmes shook it gently before, apparently satisfied that it presented no threat, examining the surfaces and removing the lid.

A leather gauntlet was revealed, its fingers torn and clotted with dried blood. He fetched a pair of tongs from his workbench and picked it up to view it from all angles.

"There is no indication of a connection with Bracken," he concluded, "or with anyone else, for that matter. Most intriguing."

After further inspection he placed it upon his workbench, to await his attention.

"Do you intend to pursue this?" I asked.

"I am sure that there is much that can be deduced from it, but it must wait. Until the shadow of Bracken is removed, neither you nor I are safe. With what we know of him, and might yet discover, we could bring about his downfall. He knows this, and will therefore do all that he can to destroy the threat that we represent."

So it was that any action on this new case was deferred. After its eventual completion, much later, I wrote the account and titled it "The Adventure of the Bloodstained Glove," which I will one day send to my publishers should Holmes grant me permission to do this.

He was adamant that we should maintain our vigilance against Bracken at all times, and that we would not be long in hearing from him.

Before much time had passed, he was proved to be correct.

The following morning, we left Baker Street as soon as breakfast was over. I was somewhat surprised at this departure from Holmes' usual attitude towards the official force, when he announced his intention to visit Scotland Yard in order to inform Inspector Hopkins about all that we had learned.

We were no more than a few minutes into our journey, when we were presented with the first evidence that our lives were still in jeopardy.

Our hansom left its straight course suddenly, careering to the other side of the street and missing an oncoming four-wheeler by inches. From the window, Holmes and I were astonished to see the body of our driver topple and fall to the ground. We found ourselves thrown from side to side, as the frightened horse galloped aimlessly on.

My breath was driven from my body as I struck the floor, and my attempts to regain my balance were frustrated by the swaying hansom. I caught a glimpse of Holmes, who had somehow lodged himself in a corner while gripping a door-handle. His top hat fell from his head but he was leaning out of the window now, his arms flailing as he attempted to grip something outside.

Then our speed lessened and he moved back inside, fighting for breath. I saw then that he had managed to grip the long reins that had been released by the driver and swept back by the motion of the coach.

We came to a gradual standstill.

"That was a narrow escape, Watson." He gasped as we got out and he went to calm the distressed horse. "Are you injured?"

"Bruises, probably. Nothing more."

"Nor I, we were most fortunate."

We tied the horse to a lamp-post and walked back to where a small crowd had gathered around the body of our driver and was being urged to disperse by a constable. Holmes explained the happening and, on recognising our names, the constable left us to summon help.

My friend, of course, lost no time in examining our unfortunate driver while I looked on.

"What killed him?" I asked. "Did the poor fellow suffer a seizure?"

Holmes turned the body onto its back and I saw at once the wound to the head.

"A shot to the temple," he observed, "but not from a firearm. The weapon that did this was an air-gun."

"I saw no one who could have fired so accurately."

"You will recall a crowd of four or five beggars, loitering near the shops back there. They are gone now, but it is certain that one of them was Bracken."

"How can we be sure of that?"

"I am aware of no other current threat to our lives, and the intention here was clearly that we should perish in a collision with another coach, or perhaps a building. He waited near our lodgings, correctly anticipating that we would emerge sooner or later to take this route."

"He seems to be uncommonly persistent."

"There is little choice for him. He believes that by now we have accumulated enough facts for the basis of a case against him, and that exposure would reveal him as a common criminal. He knows also that we would certainly have conferred, so that you have these supposed facts in your possession also. Hence, he intends to kill us both, in whatever way he can."

At that moment the constable returned with a sergeant, to whom Holmes again explained everything. A shopkeeper produced a tattered blanket, and the body was covered. We informed the two representatives of the official force that we would go immediately to Scotland Yard, to make a full report.

I hailed another hansom and we explained the fate of his colleague to the surprised driver, giving the whereabouts of our previous conveyance so that it might be retrieved. No more than fifteen minutes later we alighted outside Scotland Yard in time to encounter Inspector Hopkins, who was in the act of leaving the premises.

"Why, Mr. Holmes, Doctor Watson!" The inspector exclaimed as he saw us.

"We have much to tell you, Inspector," my friend announced.

"I was on my way to investigate a case of petty pilfering, but that can be delegated. I suggest that we repair to my office."

As we progressed down a long corridor, Hopkins called to a young man who emerged from one of the rooms. He took him aside and spoke urgently for a few minutes, before the young man nodded and respectfully took his leave.

"Young Woodhouse has recently joined the Detective Division," the inspector explained. "The case I have given to him will serve as experience."

We were soon sitting in Hopkins' office, positioned around his desk. We both refused tea and Holmes began an account of our pursuit of Bracken, which was received in patient silence until its completion.

"And how much evidence is there of this man's crimes?" Hopkins asked at last.

"Not enough to obtain a conviction, I fear," Holmes replied. "As I described, his true nature is hidden from everyone who is acquainted with him in Torquay, save Mr. Jervis and his daughter. On the surface he is of a most polite and agreeable disposition, but in truth he kills for his own convenience and possibly, on occasion, as a profession."

"You are certain that it was he who acted against you on your way here, today?"

"I am in no doubt of it."

Hopkins considered. "It may be possible to offer you some form of police protection, for a time. I will see who is available."

"Please do not trouble yourself, Hopkins. Watson and I are armed, and can protect ourselves should it prove to be necessary. We came here today to ensure that you are aware that a dangerous man is abroad in the capital. It may be that he has some purpose here, apart from his intentions towards us."

"To avoid burdening the official force, we could enlist the aid of McMurdo," I suggested to Holmes.

"I would prefer to avoid involving our prize-fighter friend, if at all possible. We will endeavour to be ready for Bracken, should he make further attempts," was the reply. "He will not find his target an easy one."

Hopkins smiled faintly. "Of that I have no doubt."

"Perhaps it would be wise to undertake a case which would take us out of London," said I.

Holmes' expression was unaltered. "Do not concern yourself overmuch, Watson. We have faced similar situations before now. I am, however, determined that we shall run this man to ground before long, and hand him over to the official force for trial."

"You will have the support of the Yard, if you need it," said Hopkins approvingly.

"My thanks to you, Hopkins. I believe that Bracken is of the view that we possess far greater evidence against him than is actually true, and it is the mounting fear of exposure that drives him to take ever greater risks."

"We can expect him to become desperate then," Hopkins concluded, "and be more prone to error in his plans."

"It is to be hoped so," Holmes replied as we rose to leave.

We engaged a four-wheeler that had delivered a group of clergymen to a nearby address, and returned to Baker Street once more. Holmes would have immediately lapsed into one of his dark reveries, had I not interrupted.

"So, what now, Holmes? Are we to remain in our rooms and wait to see what action is taken against us?"

"For a while, I think, for there are certain steps I must take. My greatest fear is for Mrs. Hudson, that she might become an accidental victim of Bracken should he employ, for example, explosives. For that reason I may take any problem that presents itself, save those that would take me out of the capital, to lead our adversary away from our lodgings."

At this, Holmes sought out our landlady and questioned her as to any callers or strangers that had come to her notice. She reported nothing but the delivery of the mid-morning post, by a postman who was known to us.

"Some delay in Bracken's further assaults would not surprise me," Holmes said after throwing himself onto the settee and spending some moments in contemplation. "I feel that this morning's attempt on our lives was a rash action, whereas he struck me as a thinking man who considers his moves with care. He has now had the opportunity to reflect upon this."

"You think he may try a more subtle approach?"

"Perhaps, but at any rate he will pause to assess the situation, if he is the sort of man I believe him to be."

"If we knew his whereabouts we could strike first, or inform Scotland Yard."

Holmes nodded. "Indeed, Watson, and there is one course I can pursue towards that."

With that he rose abruptly, and left the room. I heard his footfalls upon the stairs and saw him appear in the street below as I watched from the window. After no more than five minutes he signalled a passing street Arab and conversed with him briefly. The ragamuffin acknowledged with a quick salute before disappearing into the crowd, and Holmes returned. He sat in the armchair opposite mine around the empty fireplace, and lit his clay pipe.

"I have summoned the Irregulars. They have at least as good a chance of finding Bracken as do Hopkins and his colleagues."

There came a knock on our door and Mrs. Hudson entered with our luncheon. When we had partaken of it she returned to clear away, but in a more excited state.

"Mr. Holmes," she said with forced patience, "there is a group of..... young persons at the front door. I have said before that I would rather you did not invite them here."

"Mrs. Hudson, I have no wish to cause you distress, but perhaps you would permit just one of their number to come up to speak to us."

She glanced with disapproval at Holmes, then at me, then back to my friend. "Oh very well, one it shall be, but please oblige me by not letting these visits occur too often."

"I will endeavour to comply. Pray allow the one called Wiggins to enter."

A few minutes later the dishevelled urchin, the leader of the little band, entered our rooms and removed his tattered hat respectfully. As much information as we had about Bracken was given to him together with an initial payment for anticipated services, and he hurriedly departed. We watched from the window as the group separated, setting off in different directions to pursue their quest.

"Judging by our previous experience of them I would expect that they will certainly find Bracken, if he is still in the capital," I remarked to Holmes.

He blew out a last cloud of fragrant smoke, and knocked out his pipe. "Normally I would agree, Watson, but here we are up against a man of exceptional cunning who is as much a master of disguise as myself. However, the Irregulars will serve as best they can, as always."

With that he undertook a search of his index, followed by one of his long silences which I knew better than to disturb. I immersed myself in the newspapers, and then in a book, and it seemed but a short while before Mrs. Hudson was knocking on our door to announce dinner.

Holmes was more talkative during the meal, though not on our current situation. He commented on some scientific discoveries which threw new light, he claimed, on the origins of humanity. He was about to follow this with his observations about the developing political situation in central Europe, when a telegram arrived.

"It is from Hopkins," he said as he discarded the envelope. "He will call this evening."

The remains of dinner had long since been cleared away, and we had settled once again in our respective armchairs, when the inspector arrived.

"Hopkins!" Holmes cried in greeting. "Can we offer you a glass of port?"

The official police agent shook his head. "Not while I am pursuing my duties thank you, Mr. Holmes."

"Pray be seated, then."

Hopkins hung up his hat and settled himself.

"I have something to tell you which may be good news," he said. "A charred body has been found in Kilburn. It has been identified as that of the man you were seeking, Elijah Bracken."

My friend and I looked at each other.

"That is certain?" Holmes asked.

"As certain as we can be," the inspector replied. "He was discovered in his hotel room, where he was registered under another name."

"Has the cause of death been definitely ascertained?"

Hopkins looked bemused at this. "Why yes, it was quite obvious. A gas mantle exploded, destroying half the room and its occupant."

"You mentioned that the body was charred?"

"That is correct. It was unrecognisable."

"Then may I enquire how you can be so certain that it was that of Bracken?"

"Oh, I see the direction that your thoughts have taken, Mr. Holmes. We became aware of the dead man's identity when we searched his clothes. His morning-coat was hung on the opposite wall to where the gas mantle was situated, and fortunately escaped much of the effects of the blast and the fire. In a pocket we discovered documents belonging to one Rodney Squires-Wilton, and I recalled that you mentioned during our earlier discussion that Bracken had used that name."

"He did indeed. In Devon he has sheltered under it for years, as a well-known and respectable personage."

"His friends there will be profoundly shocked," I said, "if something of his true nature is now revealed."

"Undoubtedly," the inspector agreed. "I have already telegraphed the officer you had dealings with, Inspector Bowden, with new facts from both your visit and the Yard's enquiries. I expect to hear from him tomorrow."

Holmes nodded thoughtfully. "Hopkins, are you to return to Kilburn in the morning?"

"That was my intention, in order to ensure that nothing has been overlooked."

"Then, with your permission, Watson and I will accompany you."

I saw that the inspector was about to object, no doubt intending to remark that amateurs would not be allowed to intrude upon the business of the official force. But then his expression softened, and I knew that he was remembering that Holmes' assistance had proved invaluable to him before now.

"Very well gentlemen," he said as he rose and retrieved his hat, "I will engage a four-wheeler and call for you at nine, if that is convenient."

Holmes gave me a quick glance and received my approval.

"Thank you, Inspector, we will be ready."

#

The following morning began, surprisingly, with a letter from Inspector Bowden. This contained both a lengthy account of the amazement of all Bracken's familiars in Torquay in the light of Scotland Yard's and Holmes' discoveries and suspicions, and a profuse apology for our treatment there. Miss Jervis had come forward also, with the result that local opinion of the man who had called himself Rodney Squires-Wilton had undergone a rapid change.

"Inspector Bowden tells us that Bracken would have become a hunted man in Devon, had he lived," Holmes read. "I have more respect for the inspector now, for it is not easy for an officer of the official force to admit his error. Many are the times when I have been faced with bluster or rudeness when pointing out inconsistencies in their investigations."

"I can certainly bear witness to that," I smiled.

My friend suddenly rose and strode from the breakfast table to look down through the window. "Ah, a four-wheeler has arrived. Let us take up our hats and coats, Watson, and not keep the good inspector waiting."

We joined Hopkins and set off for Kilburn. Apart from initial greetings, little was said before we reached Kilburn High Road. I formed the impression that Inspector Hopkins was absorbed with what lay before him and was anxious to conclude the case, whereas Holmes" intended to take a more cautious approach. The coachman guided the horses into a network of side-streets, and came to a halt outside an anonymous hotel sandwiched between two dreary shops.

We gained entry to the upper floor unchallenged. The constable on duty outside the room saluted and opened the door before standing aside. We entered a blackened chamber that smelled of damp.

"I understand that the fire brigade was not called," Hopkins explained. "Several pitchers of water thrown by other guests and hotel staff were enough to quell the blaze."

"Yet the fire was sufficient to reduce the body to the condition that you described," Holmes commented.

Hopkins looked faintly embarrassed. "Apparently. The remains have, of course, been removed by now."

"A pity, but I expect this room to tell me more."

"What are you looking for, Holmes?" I asked.

"Confirmation, or the absence of it."

"But, as I said, I have seen the body. Mr. Holmes, the man was Bracken, and he was dead!" The inspector exclaimed.

"Then much of my work is already done. For my part, a short examination should suffice. I will not delay you for long."

My friend did not produce his lens or begin to take measurements within the room, in accordance with his usual methods. He merely stood in its centre, looking from the burnt-out gas mantle to the opposite wall several times before scrutinizing some of the damage.

"I think that will do," he concluded after about ten minutes. "If you are staying, Hopkins, Doctor Watson and I can easily procure a hansom."

#

As we began the return journey to our lodgings, I felt some relief that the threat of Bracken no longer hung over us. Yet Holmes had worn a perpetual frown and spoken little since leaving the hotel.

The horse slowed as we joined a procession of coaches heading in the same direction, and by the time we reached the outskirts of Kilburn I could endure the uncertainty no longer.

"Holmes, have you seen some fault in Hopkins' reconstruction of the situation in that hotel? Are you thinking that Bracken did not perish, after all?"

My friend raised his head from his chest slowly. "If only we had arrived there before the body was removed. Even a cursory examination would have been sufficient to enable me to answer you with some certainty. As it is, I am more than half convinced that Bracken's sly and deceptive nature is again at work. No doubt we will find out before too much time has passed, but for now we must continue to maintain our vigilance."

"But Hopkins insisted that he saw Bracken's body."

"I am sure that he saw *a* body, but by his own admission it was burnt beyond recognition. Does it not strike you as strange that it was found lying on the opposite side of the room to the gas burner that exploded? It was further away than the burnt bed sheets, the blackened chair or the scorched night-table, yet it sustained far greater damage. I attempted to examine the mantel for deliberate interference, but it had been warped by the heat."

I felt my uneasiness about Bracken returning. "So you believe that Bracken caused the fire in order to deceive us into thinking him dead?"

Holmes nodded his head. "To cause us to drop our guard, leaving us unsuspecting that he still awaits an opportunity to revenge himself upon us. That is the only reason he can have now for wishing our deaths, since all that he feared is now exposed. Both Hopkins and Inspector Bowden know him for what he is, and the net closes on him for his past deeds in Devon as well as London. It is possible that he plans, after removing us, to take on a new guise and resume his murderous ways elsewhere."

"To enrich himself while continuing to satisfy his sadistic appetites, without a doubt. In the course of my career I have seen both men and women who are capable of appearing normal, while living parallel lives in which they act in a completely different manner. It is a curious kind of madness."

"Indeed," Holmes agreed. "In this case the situation is worsened by Bracken's skill at altering his appearance."

I took a moment, to review our conversation. "But, all having been said, could not Hopkins be right after all? It occurs to me that the body's position could be explained by him attempting to escape from the room after absorbing the full force of the explosion, but failing to reach the door."

The hansom came to a halt near our rooms.

"Perhaps I am mistaken," Holmes replied as he took coins for the cab fare from his waistcoat pocket, "but if so let us err on the side of caution. Let us suspect and test everything, because our lives may depend upon doing so."

On Holmes' advice I maintained my safeguards and precautions, but for a full month nothing occurred to suggest that Bracken still lived.

The subject had by now featured progressively less in our conversations. Midsummer had arrived and, as we sat in comfortable silence with our newspapers one warm evening, I thought to bring it up again.

"It seems, Holmes, as if Bracken must have died in that fire after all, since we have heard nothing of him since. That is of course, unless you have neglected to tell me of some new development?"

"Not at all," my friend replied. "But I continue to recommend that we remain on our guard."

"I cannot think why, if he still lives, he has taken no further action against us. He must certainly be aware that we are waiting for any signs that he has undertaken new mischief." After a moment of reflection, I added: "Perhaps he has left London."

Holmes lowered his *Evening Standard* and sat erect in his chair. "If he still lives, that may be precisely what he means us to think. It is of course still possible that he is no longer alive, but he is a wily fox and, I suspect, a patient one. I think it unlikely that he has left the capital. Certainly he would be unwise to return to Devon, as Inspector Bowden would be only too pleased to welcome him back."

"Then he must have acquired a place where he can remain concealed, somewhere within the city or its outskirts. Doubtlessly he has made use of his skills, and changed his appearance as well as his name."

"I would be exceedingly surprised to discover otherwise."

It was about this time that Sherlock Holmes resumed his custom of accepting any new case that was sufficiently unusual to arouse his interest. He made this, his only concession to my doubts, while reminding me regularly that the affair of the Phantom Killer might not have reached its conclusion. I recall that two accounts of his work at this time, "The Adventure of the Phantom Coachman" and "The Adventure of Marcus Davery" as I have called them, were, on Holmes' instruction, consigned immediately to my box at Cox & Co., and he has only recently allowed their release for publication.

Then came the mild but overcast day when I noticed that boredom had finally clouded Holmes' disposition. For several days he had, despite my efforts, allowed long silences to pervade between minimal conversations, and I began to fear that depression would drive him once more to the cocaine bottle.

We had breakfasted and taken up our morning editions, read that which interested us and cast them aside, with my friend making no effort to fill his usual morning pipe from the dottles of yesterday. As I blew out a last smoke-cloud and put my own pipe aside, I saw with concern that he wore the most grim and solemn countenance.

"Holmes," I began, and received a sharp look in response, "it would be better for you to spend some time in the open air. Allow me to suggest a short walk, before we return here for luncheon. It is certain to lift your spirits."

"I know you mean well, Watson," he murmured, "but I have no interest in anything. I may therefore, just as well remain here. I shall tell Mrs. Hudson not to bother with luncheon for myself, for what little appetite I sometimes possess has deserted me. By all means walk the streets or one of the parks, if you feel that you will benefit from the experience, but pray leave me to my own devices."

I confess to feeling a little hurt at my friend's dismissal, and disappointed that I could think of no other inducement that might dispel his melancholy. The rattle of teacups as our landlady prepared to bring up our morning tea distracted me for a moment, before the door-bell clanged loudly. I heard her place the tray on the hall table, while answering the door.

"Holmes," I said in a last bid to raise his mood, "this could be a new client."

He took out his pocket-watch, and glanced at it gloomily. "It is the day and the hour when the butcher's boy calls."

"But no," I persisted, "someone is following Mrs. Hudson on the stairs."

At once I witnessed a startling transformation. He threw off his morose manner as if it had been a shroud, and his expression lightened. Holmes got to his feet in an agile movement and rubbed his hands together in anticipation. I felt relief flood over me, and prayed that this new case, if this indeed was such, would capture his interest.

"Mr. Thaddeus Crowley to see Mr. Holmes," announced Mrs. Hudson from the doorway. "Shall I bring tea for three, gentlemen?"

"Please do, Mrs. Hudson," said Holmes and I at almost the same instant.

She withdrew as a short and very thin man entered. Even from across the room, I could see that he was apparently suffering from a nervous affliction. A violent trembling, and the awkwardness of his movements, increased as he drew closer, so that Holmes adopted his most soothing tone in addressing him.

"Mr. Crowley, I see that you are acutely anxious about something. I am Sherlock Holmes and this is my friend and colleague, Doctor John Watson. Pray be seated and try to calm yourself, for things are rarely as bad as you imagine."

"Thank you sirs," our visitor replied in a rather high-pitched voice, and took the empty armchair.

I could see that our guest had aroused Holmes' curiosity to the point where he was observing him thoroughly. My own impression was of a physically weak man who imagined himself caught in the depths of a perpetual winter. His trembling persisted, and I found myself wondering if he could be abnormally cold-blooded -- or in the grip of overwhelming fear.

Tea was brought, and our landlady withdrew once more. I poured for all of us and we settled down to drink for a moment in silence.

"Now, Mr. Crowley," said Holmes as he replaced his half-full cup upon the nearby side-table, "if you have collected yourself sufficiently we would be interested to hear what brings you to us. Please take your time, but endeavour to omit nothing that is pertinent."

Our guest put down his own cup, and made a visible effort to stop his teeth from chattering. "I am here because I have heard that you enquire into that which is impossible."

"I have been confronted with many situations that have been described as such, but invariably the truth proves to be disappointingly ordinary when it is revealed."

"But she has threatened to kill my daughter and myself."

"Who has made this threat?"

"My wife!"

Holmes and I looked at each other, but he kept his expression mild and without dismay.

"Have you consulted the official force? Scotland Yard, for example?"

"I cannot. I would be ridiculed and dismissed."

"I doubt that this would be the first time that they have heard of such a happening," I remarked.

"No, gentlemen, you do not understand. I fear that I have not made myself clear. You see, my wife died more than a year ago."

Holmes glanced at the carpet, and then back at our visitor. I saw disappointment in my friend's face, because he had hoped for a more worthy test of his skills.

"Mr. Crowley, you must know that this cannot be. The dead remain in that state, however much we would embrace their return. If you have witnessed some sort of apparition, it can only be trickery."

"That is what I have been trying to convince myself of, but I saw her and, I tell you, I felt her cold flesh as she passed through the wall."

I saw the briefest trace of amusement pass over Holmes' face.

"Can you not see that there is already a contradiction? The apparition of your wife, you said, passed through a wall, yet she was sufficiently solid for you to touch her. An object, of whatever nature, is either solid or it is not. Ghosts, as I understand the accounts of those who claim to have seen them, are not solid but have the substance of smoke or mist."

"I think there is one account that agrees with Mr. Crowley, Holmes," I ventured.

My friend switched his gaze to me. "Pray enlighten us, Watson."

"Unless my memory is at fault, I recall a Bible passage where the crucified Jesus passes through the wall of an upper room, yet the doubting disciple Thomas was able to touch the spear wound in his side."

"Very well," Holmes said after a moment of consideration. "I suppose one cannot argue with the Good Book. You have aroused my interest, Mr. Crowley, to the extent where, rather than refer you to a priest, I will hear your account. Pray begin by telling us of yourself, for I can deduce nothing apart from the obvious facts that you have been under a great strain and that your profession involves little manual work."

Mr. Crowley gave me a puzzled look, and I explained my friend's observation. "Your hands, sir, and your clothes. The knees of your trousers, in particular."

"Of course," he murmured as understanding dawned.

"How old is your daughter?" asked Holmes with a trace of impatience.

"She will be twelve come the autumn," our visitor began. "Since the death of my wife we have remained together, living in rooms attached to the Chelsea Waxworks Museum, just off Cheyne Row, in what is known as the bohemian quarter."

"Are you the proprietor of that establishment?"

"I am, and have been so for many years. I inherited the business on the death of my father, who built it to rival Tussaud's. After the death of my wife it began to fail, probably because, in my distress, I neglected to maintain it or commission new figures. I was fortunate in meeting Mr. Septimus Dremmull, who became my partner and whose investment in the museum enabled its continuity. From then, all went well until three nights ago, when my daughter ran into my study screaming that she had seen her mother. I managed to restore her calm before asking if she had been asleep and could possibly have dreamed the incident, but she insisted that she had been reading in the sitting-room when her mother appeared before her."

"Did she furnish a description?" Holmes enquired.

"She swore that her mother wore a shroud, as if she had risen from her grave, and that it was possible to see right through her body. My daughter, whose name is Katharine, was able to keep in sight the bookcase and the wall behind the figure, as it raged and cursed and foretold that our deaths will fall within the month."

"She mentioned you both, by name?"

"She did, emphatically."

"And there have been further incidents?"

"Not involving my daughter, but I have experienced similar sightings both nights since. Katharine's description of the threats was most accurate, for they were repeated on each occasion."

"Were the words used *exactly* the same?" I asked.

Holmes, his head resting on steepled fingers, smiled. "Bravo, Watson!"

"As far as I can remember, they were," our client replied.

"You mentioned that you had actually touched the apparition," Holmes recalled. "Was that during the appearance last night?"

'It was.'

A thought occurred to me. "Forgive me, but did you notice any signs of decomposition?"

Mr. Crowley was a picture of grief. "Last night I felt her flesh. She was as cold as stone, but otherwise there was nothing different."

"And where is your daughter now?" Holmes enquired.

"At the museum. She has locked herself in her room until my return."

"Are you not afraid that the spectre will reappear?"

"She has not done so during the hours of daylight."

Holmes sat with his head upon his chest, considering the matter. He looked up suddenly.

"Mr. Crowley, what would you have us do?" he asked.

Our visitor hesitated, and then swallowed nervously. "I would be most obliged if you gentlemen would accompany me to the museum, and remain until dawn. After dinner, we could conduct a vigil together and perhaps arrive at an explanation."

Holmes gave me a questioning look, and I nodded my agreement. He sprang to his feet with a new light in his eyes.

"Very well," he took a step towards the hat-stand. "I will leave a note for Mrs. Hudson, and then we will set off immediately."

Once outside, we hailed a hansom quickly. During almost the entire journey, Mr. Crowley kept up a frantic chatter that clearly irritated Holmes. For my part I was intrigued by the man's condition, for whatever troubled him appeared not to subside for a moment, giving him no rest from his fears. Even allowing for his concern for his daughter, I had not seen such dread before.

He shifted nervously in his seat as we arrived.

"It is across the square," he shouted to our driver in a halting stammer. "The building next to the factory."

The cabby obediently brought us to a halt outside the waxworks entrance, where a large painted sign advertised some of the exhibits. When the hansom had departed and the sound of the horse's hooves grown faint, the dull repetitive impact of factory machinery was the only remaining sound. The square, a tiny enclave off Cheyne Row, would be relatively quiet until later, when the workers spilled out of the several tiny establishments to make the journey homeward.

Mr. Crowley's place of work and home was a tall building which, though square in shape, reminded me of a lighthouse. This impression was further enhanced by his explanation that the building boasted four floors, each with a flight of stairs at the far end. The quarters he shared with his daughter were situated, he told us, on the topmost level, where we would make her acquaintance.

He produced a large key that looked as if it were meant to turn the locks of a medieval castle, and opened the heavy door with some difficulty. We entered into a gloomy interior, and he closed the door behind us with a dull impact that echoed along the passage ahead.

"Each floor is a gallery of several exhibitions," he explained. "At the end we will climb to the next level where there are more, and so on until we reach the highest floor and the end of the displays. From there an additional staircase leads directly back to the ground floor and the exit to the street. That is of course where we entered just now, and is normally open at all times for customers to come and go."

"Yes, I see," said Holmes with a trace of impatience. "But tell me, on which floor did the apparition confront your daughter and yourself? Be sure to recollect accurately, for this is vital to my investigation."

At this, Mr. Crowley's uncertain demeanor intensified. This, I confess, confounded me, since his memory of the experience had been vivid until now. Holmes appeared not to notice.

"It was the topmost floor."

My friend looked at him sharply. "In every case?"

"Yes", came the reply in a trembling voice.

"In the instances of both your daughter and yourself?"

"That is what I have said."

Holmes let a long silence persist before he turned his attention to the narrow passage before us, which was half-lit by regularly-spaced gas lamps high on the wall.

"Very well, let us proceed."

As we approached the first exhibit I became aware of the strange atmosphere of the place. There was absolutely no sound, other than that of our own footsteps, for none seemed able to

119

penetrate from outside the building. Also, and it may have been my imagination, I detected a sensation of imminent evil, perhaps of murderous threat! I forced these impressions from my mind before Holmes could ask why I was thinking such things, for he had demonstrated his ability to sometimes deduce the nature of my thoughts before now.

I attempted to divert my concentration but, try as I might, I could not rid myself of a mounting unease.

We were confronted with an effigy of King Canute, unsuccessfully attempting to hold back the waves, followed by King John signing the Magna Carta.

"This is our historical section," said Mr. Crowley unnecessarily.

"Most interesting," Holmes murmured.

Because of the restriction of the rope barrier I could not get near the exhibits, but from where I stood they appeared to be works of master craftsmanship. The postures were life-like and the general appearance of the figures was such that they could easily be mistaken for living people even when viewed from a short distance. Their facial expressions and clothing gave no indications, at first sight, that these were soulless statues, fashioned in wax rather than stone. Only their stillness betrayed their true nature, or absence of it. Clever lighting enhanced the effect.

"Do you, yourself, or your daughter, possess the skill to create these images?" I asked Mr. Crowley.

He shivered, as if in the midst of extreme cold. "Good Heavens no, sir! We have workshops of skilled craftsmen who have been with us since my father's time. I am able to serve as an advisor, when new models are in the course of construction, but our factory on the other side of the capital usually produces the entire work when the subject is made known to them."

We passed an extraordinarily life-like depiction of Sir Francis Drake playing bowls at Plymouth, before ascending the first staircase.

"Here," said Mr. Crowley in his trembling voice, "we have a different subject. Behold the gods of ancient Greece!"

Holmes seemed to be paying little attention, concentrating instead on the walls and opaque windows opposite the exhibits. I, however, began to appreciate the skill that must have been required to construct the images of Zeus, Athena, Hera and many others that graced a scene from the classical conception of Mount Olympus. Despite his affliction, Mr. Crowley was clearly proud of his collection.

There were two more related exhibits on this level. A depiction of a man astride a winged horse was titled 'Pegasus and Bellerophon', and a scene made up of both summer and winter backgrounds contained a distraught young woman called 'Persephone'.

Holmes seemed unimpressed, even distracted, as we climbed to the next level. Yet I sensed a tension, an anticipation in him that echoed my own sensations. Mr. Crowley had indicated that the apparition that terrified him and his daughter appeared only after dark, so our present feelings of concern were something of a mystery to me.

This floor contained scenes of the Empire, and of the visits to its various shores by our Sovereign Lady. The depiction of her was accurate, according to the memory I have retained of a single accidental glimpse from a time when her coach passed me near Pall Mall. Holmes gazed at the effigy, lingering for longer here, before we approached the staircase that led to the highest level.

"This final floor contains a miscellany of themes," Mr. Crowley explained.

Holmes and I glanced at each other briefly, both having noticed an increase in the man's anxiety. A dark corridor led off to the left, presumably to the quarters where Mr. Crowley lived with his daughter. After that the rope barrier resumed, stretching ahead in a straight line and culminating at the end of the exhibits.

Holmes continually scrutinized everything. As before, he examined the windows and wall which faced the displays.

"This, I take it, is where your daughter and yourself witnessed the apparition?"

"It was a short way further along." Mr. Crowley's voice was now almost a whisper, but my friend appeared to attach no significance to its altered quality.

The first exhibition featured a low tank of water to represent the sea. Aboard the miniature galleon that floated upon it, battle-torn sails hung listlessly above a conflict between sailors and invading pirates. Again, the attitudes of the figures, their facial expressions and apparel appeared to me to be most realistic, and the riding of the craft upon the slight swell lent the scene a certain authenticity.

I saw that Holmes had given the depiction only cursory attention and that his movements had become cautious, as if he stalked some unseen prey. I confess to being puzzled by this, since there seemed no reason for it. Only two exhibits remained, and then we would hear from Mr. Crowley's daughter an account of her curious experience.

"Careful, Watson," Holmes murmured as Mr. Crowley went on a few paces ahead. "Keep your revolver ready."

The penultimate exhibit proved to be a bloody war scene. Though the figures of men and horses were again faithfully reproduced, I found the depiction not to my taste. Corpses, some slashed to ribbons, littered the battleground, while horsemen and their terrified mounts charged with lances and sabres to add to the carnage. A bugle boy, with a long sword piercing his body, was frozen in the act of toppling to the blood-soaked earth.

I moved on quickly after a quick perusal of the battle, to join Holmes who had already done so.

At last we were confronted with the final exhibition. We looked with some surprise at a dark and strangely disquieting circus scene.

This display was different, for a taxidermist had evidently supplied the waxworks with lions, tigers and a single leopard. In the background a group of clowns looked on from the shadows, some laughing while others hung arrested in the act of somersaulting. One wore a grotesque smile and seemed to follow our movements with his eyes. The centre of the scene was a sawdust ring, dominated by a tall ringmaster holding, not a whip, but, to my surprise, a flickering candle. He wore a long coat and an absurd pink top hat, with a mask covering the upper part of his face. I saw cruelty in the curve of his mouth, and a hint of madness. I turned to ask Mr. Crowley what could have inspired such an odd portrayal, but to my surprise he was no longer to be seen! Holmes and I turned as one to see the stout door behind us, one of those placed at intervals in case of fire but normally left open, slammed hard and locked. We heard Mr. Crowley's laboured breathing beyond it, but apart from that there was silence.

"This is what I have been expecting," Holmes said. "Be prepared to shoot to kill."

We turned back to the exhibit. Somehow I felt that it looked darker than before, and had acquired a sinister element. I was about to dismiss the notion, then I peered again at the strange figure of the ringmaster. I shrugged and turned to speak to Holmes then, realising what I had missed, turned quickly back.

"You saw it, Watson?"

"I did. The statue's eyes moved. They blinked."

We drew our weapons simultaneously. At the same moment the ringmaster threw off his hat and ripped away the mask, grinning at us insanely.

"Good day, Mr. Bracken," Holmes said at once.

"Holmes, that is not Bracken!" I retorted. "He does not resemble the man we met in Devon."

"Again you forget, Watson, his considerable skill at the art of disguise. Look at his face. The hair and moustache are different, but he cannot alter the shape of his head or the way he stands."

I saw that he was correct. "You expected this?"

"Not at first, but when Mr. Crowley related that ridiculous story it was apparent to me that someone badly wished for our presence here. All others who came to mind are currently in prison."

"No, you could not have known," Bracken's voice was higher-pitched than I remembered, almost shrill. "My plan was perfect, for here you are. You are no match for me, Mr. Sherlock Holmes."

"Yet it is you, and not I, who have become a fugitive and cannot return to his home. As for your identity, the deduction was a simple one."

The echo of Holmes' voice died away, and I saw a strange glint in Bracken's eyes that convinced me that the exposing of his criminal past had indeed had an effect upon his sanity.

"Yet in a way, it has all been worthwhile," he said in a wistful tone. "I have killed for pleasure and for profit, and always there is a supreme satisfaction. The hunt is the essence of life. I could never have endured the monotonous life of the everyday fellow."

"Was it pleasure or profit that sealed the fate of Mr. Stephen Golding and his sister?" enquired Holmes.

Bracken shrugged. "It was a debt I had to repay, from my time in Africa."

"Are you proposing that we should all perish in a fire?" I asked him, indicating the candle that he held.

He looked at the flame as if he had forgotten it was there. "No, I have different intentions." He held up his other hand, which held what appeared to be a length of thin rope that disappeared into the shadows. "Put down your weapons, gentlemen, or I will immediately ignite this fuse."

"It cannot have escaped your notice," Holmes said calmly, "that if you have installed explosives in this building, you will meet the same fate as us."

"Not so," Bracken allowed himself a superior smirk. "How you continue to underestimate my talents. It will appear, to the likes of Scotland Yard, that I have indeed perished here, but I shall once again adopt another name and another life. But no, if this fuse burns it will be our friend Mr. Crowley's daughter, confined to a locked room, who will be blasted out of existence."

"Extinguish the candle," I ordered, "or we will fire before you can act."

"I think not." He brought the flame and the fuse closer together. "I have carefully tested the fuse. It burns rapidly. Miss Crowley would be dead before my body hit the floor."

"How can you call yourself a gentleman?" I asked bitterly.

He gave a short, hysterical laugh. "Perhaps I will be, yet again. You saw at the Sirius Club that I mix well with their like. Now, drop your firearms to the floor." He hesitated, as a new thought occurred to him. "No, Wait! Doctor Watson, throw down your revolver. Mr. Holmes, point your weapon away from me."

"Obey him, Watson," Holmes said in a low voice.

As my revolver fell to the floor, I glanced at my friend. I think we both anticipated what was to come.

"Now we can proceed," Bracken said cheerfully. "Mr. Holmes, aim your weapon and shoot Doctor Watson in the head."

Holmes looked at him sharply.

"It will be a supreme irony," Bracken continued, "when you are hanged for murder while I become, once again, a free man."

Holmes stood very still, and for a moment there was complete silence. Then a grim smile spread across his face, and he began to walk calmly towards Bracken.

"No, Holmes!" I cried. "I beg of you, do not sacrifice that child's life for mine!"

"Do not be alarmed, old fellow," he said as he approached our adversary. "There is nothing to fear."

As he drew nearer, Bracken brought the flame and the fuse closer in a threatening gesture. With a single sweep of his arm Holmes dashed the candle to the floor, where it immediately went out. A revolver was drawn and immediately shaken free as, in an instant, Holmes held Bracken's arm in the steely grip that I had seen him use to restrain criminals before. He then whipped a pair of police handcuffs from his pocket and secured his adversary's hands behind his back.

"Holmes," I gasped with relief, "you took an enormous risk."

"Very much to the contrary," he said, as he bent to pick up the fuse. To my amazement it was nothing but a piece of rope, about six or seven feet in length and connected to nothing.

Bracken, who by now I was certain was quite mad, laughed like an unruly schoolboy caught playing a prank.

"A trick! But how did you know?" I asked Holmes.

"The question presented no great difficulty. He was relying on our concern for the girl to prevent us from analysing the situation. It took me but a moment to calculate how far the fuse would have to burn, even to leave this room. In addition to the fact that there would have been plenty of time to stamp it out, or sever it with my pocket-knife, its apparent path was set in the wrong direction to reach the Crowley's apartment." Our prisoner struggled, but Holmes tightened his grip. "He spoke of rapid burning, but to achieve that effect the fuse has to be soaked in a special heat-enhancing chemical such as is used by the military.

Had it been prepared in this way, the resulting strong smell would have been apparent."

As I had done many times before, I marvelled at my friend's powers of observation and reasoning. "If he had drawn his weapon, Holmes, he could have killed us both."

"No, I realised that such a straightforward revenge would be unsatisfactory to him. He would have taken so much more pleasure in forcing me to commit murder and become a hunted man, thus changing places with him when he disappeared and adopted a new identity."

I nodded. "He was always the deceiver."

"Precisely. But now I think we must be getting along. Inspector Hopkins will be glad to hear from us, I should think, and the hangman will be waiting after the trial."

He attempted to lead Bracken away, but our prisoner stood firm. I watched as he whispered something that I failed to catch, and I saw a look of surprise pass quickly over Holmes' face.

"It will not do," he said to Bracken. "Scotland Yard is close behind him. He will be hard put to, if he is to save even himself."

I resolved to ask my friend about this conversation later. We left with Bracken between us, staring dejectedly at the floor, but after several paces he tore himself from our grasp and ran ahead. I could easily have caught him but, to my surprise, Holmes put a hand on my arm to hold me back.

We looked on as Bracken, his hands manacled behind him, dived like an expert swimmer through one of the opaque windows and disappeared from our sight.

A horrible cry reached us, then a sickening impact. We broke away more of the glass and peered down, to see Bracken splayed upon the road amidst a spreading pool of blood. A horse, pulling a loaded cart, reared in terror while its driver tried to calm it, as a few people from the surrounding buildings gathered around the corpse.

"We could have prevented that," I said in some dismay.

"Justice was better served, Watson, I promise you. I will explain fully later. For now, we must re-acquaint ourselves with Mr. Crowley."

"Bracken's co-conspirator?"

"I hardly think so."

"But he locked us in here, to be murdered."

"He had little choice, and has been punished enough."

I said no more, but Holmes and I pounded on the locked door. After receiving no response Holmes became impatient and I, having retrieved my revolver, joined him in shooting at the lock until it fell to the floor. We emerged with caution that was found to be unnecessary, and then retraced our steps until we reached the corridor leading to Mr. Crowley's private quarters.

At its end we stood outside the door and listened. There was only silence within. Then we heard a low murmuring and Holmes rapped upon the oak panels and waited. We heard no movement but the sound continued and I opened the unlocked door slowly. We entered a spacious sitting room where Mr. Crowley sat upon a couch with his arms around his daughter. They were praying.

Mr. Crowley looked up as he heard us approach, then gave his daughter a final hug and got to his feet. I saw at once that most of the fear had gone from his face, replaced by an expression of sad resignation.

"I know, gentlemen, what to expect," he said seriously. "I have committed a grave crime and must be punished. I will give you no further trouble, but I do not know how to begin to apologise for placing your lives in such danger. If I could excuse myself, it would be on the grounds of protecting my daughter, for Dremmull instructed me on your deception and threatened to ensure that Katharine suffered a horrible death if I deviated in the slightest degree from his orders."

"You knew that man as your benefactor?" I enquired.

"At first, then as my business partner. However, his true intentions soon became clear, as did his true nature."

"This was his refuge, when in London." Holmes observed.

"Yes, indeed," Mr. Crowley turned to glance at his daughter, a pretty child who watched us with frightened, red-rimmed eyes. "He came here when the mood took him. He was a violent man, who terrified us with stories of his past that I am sure were true. I had no doubt also that he would carry out his threats if either of us attempted to expose him." He looked down at the carpeted floor and then at Holmes. "I assume he is no more, or you would not be here."

"Bracken, for that is his true name, will take no further lives."

Mr. Crowley sighed heavily. "Very well, it is time to leave. May I prevail upon you gentlemen to make some attempt to settle Katharine at an orphanage, or to see her with some loving, childless couple?"

There followed what seemed to me to be a long silence. Holmes' face was set like flint, and I wondered if, uncharacteristically, he intended to inflict some punishment of his own for Mr. Crowley's part in springing Bracken's trap.

Then my friend's eyes fell on the child and, for an instant, I saw in his face the compassion that lay beneath his unemotional exterior.

"You, yourself, shall take care of your daughter, Mr. Crowley," he said in a voice that was not unkind. "Come, Watson, we have much to report to Scotland Yard."

130

I glanced back as I closed the door behind us, to see intense relief on Mr. Crowley's surprised face.

We hailed a hansom in Cheyne Row. On the way to Scotland Yard, Holmes proved to be uncharacteristically communicative.

"When did you realise that Mr. Crowley's revelations were nothing but a deception?" I asked him as we rattled through cobbled streets.

He smiled, reflectively. "You know well, Watson, that I have little belief in the supernatural. On each occasion that such a problem has been presented to us, the eventual solution has proved to be little out of the ordinary."

"So you have always maintained."

"Quite so. Thus, when Mr. Crowley told his story of malevolent ghosts passing through walls, I at first considered that he was the victim of trickery or that his objective was to induce us to leave Baker Street to allow something to take place in our absence. However, I soon concluded that his most likely reason was probably to arouse our interest so that we would accompany him to the waxworks."

"Did you dismiss your concern regarding our lodgings?"

"Not at all. I was uncertain, at this time, as to whether this new matter might involve Bracken, but I had not forgotten the threat he represented. It was possible that Mrs. Hudson could have been injured or killed or our rooms damaged, while we were away. I therefore left a note for her, as you may recall. It contained instructions to telegraph the private enquiry agent Barker, whom I have used from time to time."

"So that he would watch Baker Street and observe any suspicious activities, in our absence?"

"And possibly take action, though I considered it an unlikely necessity on reflection. I then asked myself why, if for reasons of his own, Mr. Crowley would tell such an unbelievable story. Why not, for example, simply say there had been a burglary? It occurred to me then that this summons could be from someone who knew that it is the cases with unusual features that I find most attractive, whereas I might recommend a client with an ordinary problem to Scotland Yard."

"And it was then that you suspected that Bracken had reappeared, to take his revenge?"

Holmes glanced out of the window, as a child chased a ball across the road ahead. "As I mentioned previously, any of my past opponents who were likely to have concocted such a scheme are behind bars, or dead. My examination of the walls, opposite the wax exhibits, finally confirmed that there was no trickery or other possibility that any solid substance could have passed through them. You will remember that, at this point, I reminded you to keep your revolver ready. As Bracken was pleased to tell us, his method of revenge on us for exposing his activities in Devon and elsewhere, was to compel me to murder you and to hang for it. I have no doubt that his warped sense of irony would have been satisfied by this."

"Nor have I," I agreed. "But tell me, Holmes, what was it that Bracken whispered to you as we led him away from the circus exhibit? It appeared to be some sort of last hope for escape."

He laughed shortly. "Indeed it was. He confided in me that he is distantly related to Sir Roger Ballingham who, he boasted with certainty, would extricate him from the clutches of the law."

"Sir Roger Ballingham? The cousin of the Duke of __"

"Precisely. That is what Bracken claimed, to induce me to release him. It is known that Sir Roger himself is no stranger to scandal, or to crime, although his activities have been concealed until now for the sake of the family reputation."

"As I recall, gambling was at the root of his misdeeds."

"Indeed. The Duke would cover his debts no more, so he took to crime. Several detectives at Scotland Yard are watching Sir Roger closely, but no more than that as yet. However, I must confess that I exaggerated a little when I told Bracken that Sir Roger was in no position to help him."

"So that was why, his last hope of escape from the hangman gone, he took his own life. You employed a slight deception of your own there, I think. I suppose you could view it as beating Bracken at his own game."

"I could not allow him to walk feely in the streets of London again, Watson. He has taken too many lives, and would doubtlessly have taken more. Heaven knows the true extent of his guilt."

I nodded. "There are probably many unsolved crimes that should be laid at his door."

"I recall that Alfred Court said as much."

Holmes' expression brightened as the driver brought the hansom to rest outside the entrance to Scotland Yard. "And now we will relate all this to Inspector Hopkins, enriching his day with the knowledge that some of his outstanding cases need trouble him no more and securing the speedy release of Mr. Janner, whose unjust imprisonment began the sequence of events that destroyed one of the most unrepentant criminals that I have so far encountered."

Also from MX Publishing

MX Publishing is the world's largest specialist Sherlock Holmes publisher, with over a hundred titles and fifty authors creating the latest in Sherlock Holmes fiction and non-fiction.

From traditional short stories and novels to travel guides and quiz books, MX Publishing cater for all Holmes fans.

The collection includes leading titles such as *Benedict Cumberbatch In Transition* and *The Norwood Author* which won the 2011 Howlett Award (Sherlock Holmes Book of the Year).

MX Publishing also has one of the largest communities of Holmes fans on Facebook with regular contributions from dozens of authors.

www.mxpublishing.com

Also from MX Publishing

Our bestselling books are our short story collections;

"Lost Stories of Sherlock Holmes" , "The Outstanding
Mysteries of Sherlock Holmes", The Papers of Sherlock
Holmes Volume 1 and 2, "Untold Adventures of Sherlock
Holmes" (and the sequel "Studies in Legacy) and "Sherlock
Holmes in Pursuit", "The Cotswold Werewolf and Other
Stories of Sherlock Holmes" – and many more......

www.mxpublishing.com

Also from MX Publishing

"Phil Growick's, "The Secret Journal of Dr. Watson", is an adventure which takes place in the latter part of Holmes and Watson's lives. They are entrusted by HM Government (although not officially) and the King no less to undertake a rescue mission to save the Romanovs, Russia's Royal family from a grisly end at the hand of the Bolsheviks. There is a wealth of detail in the story but not so much as would detract us from the enjoyment of the story. Espionage, counter-espionage, the ace of spies himself, double-agents, double-crossers...all these flit across the pages in a realistic and exciting way. All the characters are extremely well-drawn and Mr. Growick, most importantly, does not falter with a very good ear for Holmesian dialogue indeed. Highly recommended. A five-star effort."
The Baker Street Society

www.mxpublishing.com

Also from MX Publishing

The Missing Authors Series

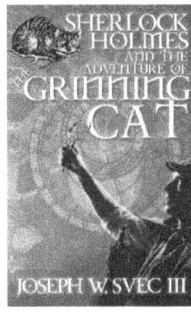

Sherlock Holmes and The Adventure of The Grinning Cat
Sherlock Holmes and The Nautilus Adventure
Sherlock Holmes and The Round Table Adventure

"Joseph Svec III is brilliant in entwining two endearing and enduring classics of literature, blending the factual with the fantastical; the playful with the pensive; and the mischievous with the mysterious. We shall, all of us young and old, benefit with a cup of tea, a tranquil afternoon, and a copy of Sherlock Holmes, The Adventure of the Grinning Cat."
Amador County Holmes Hounds Sherlockian Society

Also from MX Publishing

The American Literati Series

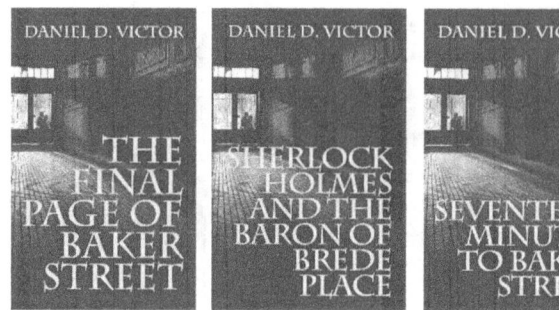

The Final Page of Baker Street
The Baron of Brede Place
Seventeen Minutes To Baker Street

"The really amazing thing about this book is the author's ability to call up the "essence" of both the Baker Street "digs" of Holmes and Watson as well as that of the "mean streets" of Marlowe's Los Angeles. Although none of the action takes place in either place, Holmes and Watson share a sense of camaraderie and self-confidence in facing threats and problems that also pervades many of the later tales in the Canon. Following their conversations and banter is a return to Edwardian England and its certainties and hope for the future. This is definitely the world before The Great War."
Philip K Jones

www.mxpublishing.com

Also from MX Publishing

The Detective and The Woman Series

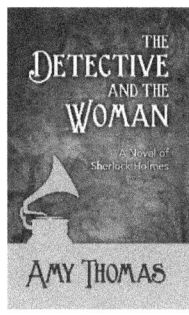  

The Detective and The Woman
The Detective, The Woman and The Winking Tree
The Detective, The Woman and The Silent Hive

"The book is entertaining, puzzling and a lot of fun. I believe the author has hit on the only type of long-term relationship possible for Sherlock Holmes and Irene Adler. The details of the narrative only add force to the romantic defects we expect in both of them and their growth and development are truly marvelous to watch. This is not a love story. Instead, it is a coming-of-age tale starring two of our favorite characters."
Philip K Jones

www.mxpublishing.com

Also from MX Publishing

The Sherlock Holmes and Enoch Hale Series

The Amateur Executioner
The Poisoned Penman
The Egyptian Curse

"The Amateur Executioner: Enoch Hale Meets Sherlock Holmes", the first collaboration between Dan Andriacco and Kieran McMullen, concerns the possibility of a Fenian attack in London. Hale, a native Bostonian, is a reporter for London's Central News Syndicate - where, in 1920, Horace Harker is still a familiar figure, though far from revered. "The Amateur Executioner" takes us into an ambiguous and murky world where right and wrong aren't always distinguishable. I look forward to reading more about Enoch Hale."
Sherlock Holmes Society of London

www.mxpublishing.com

Also from MX Publishing

Sherlock Holmes novellas in verse

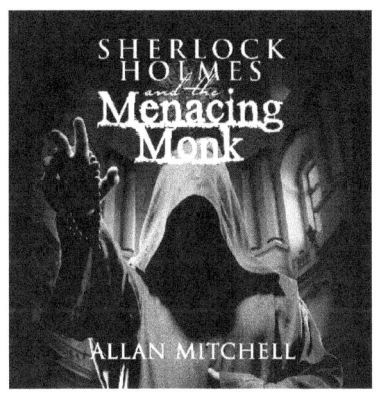

All four novellas
have been
released also in
audio format
with narration
by Steve White

Sherlock Holmes and The Menacing Moors
Sherlock Holmes and The Menacing Metropolis
Sherlock Holmes and The Menacing Melbournian
Sherlock Holmes and The Menacing Monk

*"The story is really good and the Herculean effort it must have been to write it all in verse — well, my hat is off to you, Mr.. Allan Mitchell! I wouldn't dream of seeing such work get less than five plus stars from me…"***The Raven**

Also from MX Publishing

When the papal apartments are burgled in 1901, Sherlock Holmes is summoned to Rome by Pope Leo XII. After learning from the pontiff that several priceless cameos that could prove compromising to the church, and perhaps determine the future of the newly unified Italy, have been stolen, Holmes is asked to recover them. In a parallel story, Michelangelo, the toast of Rome in 1501 after the unveiling of his Pieta, is commissioned by Pope Alexander VI, the last of the Borgia pontiffs, with creating the cameos that will bedevil Holmes and the papacy four centuries later. For fans of Conan Doyle's immortal detective, the game is always afoot. However, the great detective has never encountered an adversary quite like the one with whom he crosses swords in "The Vatican Cameos."

"An extravagantly imagined and beautifully written Holmes story"
(Lee Child, NY Times Bestselling author, Jack Reacher series)